The King's Nun

Also by Catherine Monroe

The Barefoot Girl

The King's Nun

Catherine Monroe

New American Library

New American Library
Published by New American Library, a division of
Penguin Group (USA) Inc., 375 Hudson Street,
New York, New York 10014, USA
Penguin Group (Canada), 90 Eglinton Avenue East, Suite 700, Toronto,
Ontario M4P 2Y3, Canada (a division of Pearson Penguin Canada Inc.)
Penguin Books Ltd., 80 Strand, London WC2R 0RL, England
Penguin Ireland, 25 St. Stephen's Green, Dublin 2,
Ireland (a division of Penguin Books Ltd.)
Penguin Group (Australia), 250 Camberwell Road, Camberwell, Victoria 3124,
Australia (a division of Pearson Australia Group Pty. Ltd.)
Penguin Books India Pvt. Ltd., 11 Community Centre, Panchsheel Park,
New Delhi - 110 017, India
Penguin Group (NZ), cnr Airborne and Rosedale Roads, Albany,
Auckland 1310, New Zealand (a division of Pearson New Zealand Ltd.)
Penguin Books (South Africa) (Pty.) Ltd., 24 Sturdee Avenue,
Rosebank, Johannesburg 2196, South Africa

Penguin Books Ltd., Registered Offices: 80 Strand, London WC2R 0RL, England

First published by New American Library, a division of Penguin Group (USA) Inc.

First Printing, January 2007
1 3 5 7 9 10 8 6 4 2

Cover painting: *Saint Magdalene Reading.* Louvre, Paris. © Erich Lessing/Art Resource, NY

NEW AMERICAN LIBRARY and logo are trademarks of Penguin Group (USA) Inc.

LIBRARY OF CONGRESS CATALOGING-IN-PUBLICATION DATA:
Monroe, Catherine.
The king's nun / Catherine Monroe.
p. cm.
ISBN-13: 978-0-451-22019-6
1. Nuns—Fiction. 2. Charlemagne, Emperor, 742-814—Fiction. 3. Germany—
History—To 843—Fiction. I. Title.
PS3613.O5367K56 2007
813'.6—dc22 2006017241

Set in Giovanni • Designed by Elke Sigal

Printed in the United States of America

Acknowledgments

With special thanks to Eileen Stanton,
my premier authority on Catholicism.

I

MÜNSTER-BILZEN ABBEY

AUTUMN–SPRING, 793–794 ANNO DOMINI

Amelia

He came to me out of the mists that cloak the forests of the Ardennes. It is a wild area, heavy with trees, sheer rocky cliffs, deep canyons, and dark and secret caves, where, it is said, goddesses once lived.

When I first saw him, he was nothing more than a shimmering darkness, undulating and without form in a shroud of vapor. The apparition brought me to a halt as I walked along the path that leads from the abbey to the forest, where I often went to gather herbs. I watched until a man on horseback materialized out of the swarming opaque mass. He was a giant of a man, tall, with a broad span of shoulders and a large head. His hair was the color of spun copper and curled about his face, which was ruddy of complexion, and possessed of a large nose. He wore the linen shirt and breeches as well as the short leather boots of a commoner, and he rode astride a sorrel gelding eighteen hands high. A dead stag was flung across the back of the horse behind the rider.

I myself was shrouded in the foggy mists, and he failed to see me at first. He was about to ride past me when he pulled his reins. The horse's enormous nostrils flared, and I could feel his hot breath on my face. His fine mane billowed as his head danced in response to the rider's pull.

Without a word, the man leaned over in his saddle and offered his thick, muscular arm to me. I took it without question, as if I knew he was my destiny, and allowed him to raise me up until I was seated behind him, wedged between the man and the stag. My arms could not fully encircle his girth, but I couldn't help but enjoy the warmth of him, for it was autumn, and a chill had seeped through my cloak. The masculine smell of him and the feel of his strong body beneath his shirt were new to me. I hadn't told him whence I came nor where I was headed, but he must have guessed by my simple white woolen habit, secured with a rope at my waist, that I was from the abbey, for that is where he took me.

He dismounted at the gate, helped me down, and spoke for the first time—words that seemed so odd as to be incomprehensible.

"You are mine, little nun."

I watched him as he rode away and thought of him almost constantly for several days until his memory was draped and hidden by the mists of passing weeks and by the demands of my life at the abbey.

My mother and father gave me to Münster-Bilzen Abbey, along with a considerable sum that would have been my inheritance, as a gift to God, before I shed all of my milk teeth. I had lived there since my seventh birthday, which, on the autumn day this story begins, had been a month past ten years ago.

The abbess was Mother Landrada, whom I loved and had come to think of as my true mother. I had never disobeyed her, although I had argued with her a few times, as mother and daughter are wont to do.

On the day she asked me to greet and escort the king during his visit to the abbey, I was sorely tempted to disobey. I had never met the king and had no desire to meet him. It would pull me away from my books, and I would be forced to be charming, deferential, and above all, quiet, except when I was required to give an answer.

Mother Landrada spoke. "My dear Amelia, you know I would prefer to escort him myself, but I'm not well. You must've noticed how short of breath I've become, and my limbs are so swollen movement is difficult for me, so I give you the honor of showing His Majesty the abbey."

She was a sturdy woman, florid of face, big of bone and bosom like many Saxon women. She was also elderly, nearing fifty, I believe. Her hands were red at the joints and stiff with swelling, and I could see a puffy ankle just below the hem of her robe. Her labored breath made a noisy liquid sound in her chest, and I felt a gnawing stab of sadness to see her that way. Since she was a lay abbess, I was not required to address her as Mother, as I would have been if she were a nun. Nevertheless, because of my love for her, it had become my custom to use that address with her, as it had with many of the others who called Münster-Bilzen home.

"You honor me, Mother, but I'm not worthy." I spoke with my eyes downcast. "May I suggest that Sister Ravenna would be more—"

"Sister Ravenna does not speak the Francique tongue well enough, and the king prefers to converse in that language. I will see him, of course, and I will speak to him in private, but I will rely on you to show him the abbey so he can witness our great need with his own eyes."

I was silent for a moment, no more than a second or two, while I weighed what, if anything, I should say. Should I feign a humble attitude and insist I was neither capable nor worthy of the task? Should I tell her my menses were due and I would, therefore, be indisposed? Could I think of a better excuse?

"Mother Landrada, I'm afraid—" I had started to speak before I knew what I would say, and she interrupted me.

"Don't argue with me, Amelia."

"But I wasn't going to—"

"Yes, you were. You seem always to argue, testing everything I say to you. When will you learn obedience?"

Once again I dropped my gaze. "I'm sorry, Mother. Of course, I shall be happy to escort the king for you."

She breathed a heavy, weary sigh, and the rattling in her chest was even louder. "Amelia, Amelia, don't you understand how important this is? This is the *king*. No, not just the king. This is Charles, king of the Franks and favored by the Holy Father."

"I'm truly sorry, Mother." I still kept my head down, though I wanted with all my heart to look her in the eye and tell her it mattered not a whit to me who was king or whether or not he was favored by the pope. The most important thing to me was to finish reading Vitruvius's manuscript on construction and architecture, because I still had yet to read Boethius's works on arithmetic as well as another work I'd found on agriculture. I wanted to learn all I could of such practical matters. It was, I believed, my calling to become abbess of Münster-Bilzen Abbey.

Landrada's ample bosom heaved with another heavy sigh. "You must learn obedience and self-discipline, Amelia, especially if you will someday take the veil, and even more so if you will follow in the footsteps of your holy and sainted aunt to become abbess of Münster-Bilzen."

She was speaking of my kinswoman, also called Landrada, who was a nun and the founding abbess of Münster-Bilzen more than a hundred years ago. She is now Saint Landrada, having been canonized by His Holiness Pope Gregory. The woman who spoke to me now took her name in recognition of my kinswoman's piety.

The current Landrada leveled her gaze on me. "You will go to your cell and read the psalms continuously for the remainder of the day until compline. You will pray through the hour of sext without your lunch and through vespers without your supper." She waved one of her swollen hands as if to shoo me out of her office. "Go now, Amelia. Do your penance, and I expect to see you in the chapel with the nuns for prayers tomorrow morning at two and a half hours past midnight. His Majesty's messenger has sent word that the king will be here shortly after daybreak."

There was nothing to do but obey. I bent my body in a deep bow before her and turned to walk out with my eyes still downcast. May God forgive me, but what I really wanted to do was to rant in protest because continuous reading of the psalms until compline meant at least six hours lost when I couldn't read and study the books I'd selected.

I had a great interest in all the aspects of the abbey, from the architectural plan and construction to the accounts, the maintenance and proliferation of the library, and the cultivation of the lands. To be able to understand completely all that is Münster-Bilzen, I needed to learn as much as I could, not only of Vitruvius's ideas on architecture, but of agriculture and the arithmetic of accounting procedures and countless other subjects.

My hope of following in the footsteps of both Landradas to become abbess was not, I hoped, a sinful ambition. I did truly want to serve God by becoming the best abbess I could be. I would not be a lay abbess, but a nun. I had already begun my novitiate. Of course I knew that Mother Landrada was right, that I must learn obedience. But must I learn it at that moment? Couldn't it wait at least until after I finished Vitruvius's manuscript?

It was a poor decision on my part to sneak back into the library to continue my studies. I found it was hard for me to concentrate on Vitruvius's discourse on the radius of a column's base and its equality to a demimodule. I had to read the same paragraph over and over again to understand how Pythagoras's theorem would help avoid problems in deviations of a structure, and how to avoid irrational numbers in dimensions by using near squares. While it all should have been simple enough to absorb, guilt clouded my brain. All I could think of was that I should be reading the psalms.

I got back to my cell several hours later than I would have had I obeyed Mother Landrada. Located in the novices' dormitory, a long wooden building a short walk from the church, my cell, like all the others, was small. If I were to prostrate myself on the wooden floor, I would not be able to stretch my arms in front of me in any direction. There was a minuscule window near the top. A narrow bed and a small table were the only furnishings.

In order to assuage my guilt, I stayed awake to read the psalms well past the time I should have been sleeping, in the hope that I could redeem my soul. That meant I'd been asleep a mere two hours when the nun who rang the bell for vigilia made her way through the darkened dormitory, as she did every morning at two and a half hours past midnight. I, along with the others, had to arise from bed to pray and recite the psalms in the church.

The droning voices and the warmth provided by all the bodies in the chapel were numbing. I knew I'd fallen asleep on my knees when I awoke with a jerk just as my body was toppling forward. Sister Adolpha, who was praying next to me, turned her bowed head toward me and gave me a questioning frown. I went back to chanting the psalms, but I'd hardly recited two lines when I felt myself drifting again. A jab in the ribs by Sister Adolpha's sharp elbow brought me back suddenly from that pleasant state. When I turned to look at her, she gave me a warning look.

Thank God for Sister Adolpha. If Landrada was like a mother to me, then Adolpha had become my sister. She possessed a remarkable intellect and was one of the few women at Münster-Bilzen with whom I could have a true conversation. Best of all, perhaps, was that I could trust her never to let me do something as dreadful as falling on my face during the recitation of the psalms at vigiliae.

When at last the psalms and prayers were over, all of us walked single file out of the church. Adolpha was in front of me, but as soon as we were out the door, she slowed her walk and, without looking at me, waited for me to catch up with her.

"What's wrong with you?" she whispered.

"Not enough sleep." I, too, spoke in a whisper. It is not forbidden for us to speak to one another, but we are warned not to indulge in idle chatter nor to raise our voices.

"I guessed as much. The question is why?"

I didn't answer her immediately, knowing it was best

that others not hear what I had to confess. I waited until we were well into the courtyard, where we were expected to meditate until matins.

"Mother Landrada gave me a penance for being argumentative. I was awake all night reading the psalms." We were strolling around the dark courtyard with our heads down as we spoke. Others around us strolled or sat in meditation on the wooden benches or under the great trees that hovered overhead and hid their burgeoning buds in the cool darkness.

Adolpha kept her head bowed and didn't speak for several seconds. When she spoke, it was only one word, spoken as a question.

"And . . . ?"

"And what?" I pretended ignorance.

"And what's the rest of the story? Landrada may require us to pray through supper, but she expects even the most disobedient to be in bed immediately after compline."

That wasn't the first time Adolpha's acute perception had allowed her to see inside my soul. Perhaps it was because she knew me so well. She was the first person I met when I arrived at Münster-Bilzen Abbey. She must be the same age as I, although she had already been there two years when I arrived. She seemed always to be ahead of me. She came to her decision to become a bride of Christ long before I did and had already passed through her novitiate and taken the veil.

"Do you question extreme devotion?" I asked in what I

must have already known would be a vain attempt to throw her off.

"Extreme devotion? Or extreme guilt? What sin do you have on your conscience?" Adolpha had a way of being direct without being offensive. There was no hint of condemnation in her voice.

By now my head felt as if it were floating free of my body, and I had an ache between my eyes as well as a gnawing in my stomach. The cool air made me shiver, and all I could think of was that we still had to get through matins before we could break our fast.

"Amelia?" Once again Adolpha brought me out of my fog. I had forgotten to answer her. And now I had forgotten her question.

"Are you never tempted by sin, Adolpha?" I said finally.

"Of course. It is God's way of testing us."

I couldn't see her in the darkness, but I knew she was the picture of purity—small and fragile, almost like a doll. Her skin, where it showed around her wimple, was the color and texture of the palest rose petal, and her eyes, framed by lashes that were almost invisible, were the color of faded wisteria. I could not imagine her being tempted by any sin, least of all giving in to it.

"My guilt is because I put the knowledge of the world above the sanctity of prayer," I said, too tired now to be elusive.

"Oh, of course. I should have guessed," Adolpha said, giving me a secret smile. "You went to the library to read instead of to your cell to read the Bible and pray, and then you felt you had to make recompense."

"Yes," I said with a heavy sigh. "You are right. You are always right. I am darkness and you are light."

I often thought of the two of us that way, since, while I, like her, am small of bone, and I suppose some would even call me fragile, I am not rose-petal pale. Instead, I have dark eyes and hair and skin the color of yellow cream.

She sputtered, and I knew she was laughing at what I'd just said, but she covered it by pretending to sneeze. "You are overly dramatic, my dear sister," she said under her breath. "More so than usual. Lack of sleep brings out the worst in all of us."

That last remark, which I took as criticism, made me feel cross, but before I could think of a suitable retort, she spoke again.

"If you can make it through matins, then you can go back to the library after breakfast. The library is a perfect place to sleep."

"Would that were the case. But alas, Mother Landrada has other plans for me. I am to be the king's escort as he tours Münster-Bilzen."

Adolpha stopped dead still, and I sensed her looking at me. "The king?"

"Shhh," I said, trying to keep my voice as well as my head down. Adolpha had spoken just loud enough that I feared others would be able to tell we were conversing rather than praying or meditating. "Yes, the king," I whispered.

"King Charles? You are to escort His Majesty King Charles?"

"Why are you so in awe?" My lack of sleep was making me feel cross, and I'm afraid it showed in my voice. "It's not as if he is our Lord Jesus Christ."

"Have you any idea of his power?" I would swear she sounded scornful.

"Why should I concern myself with his power?" It is amazing how hunger and lack of sleep can put such a bite in one's voice.

She stopped walking and looked at me. "Is *that* what caused you to be disrespectful to the abbess? Because she wants you to escort the king?" At least she kept her voice down.

"Apparently it's a matter of importance to you. In that case, why don't you go to Mother Landrada and volunteer to take my place?" I was feeling and sounding even more disgruntled.

Adolpha looked at me in silence for a few seconds. She wore an odd expression on her face, one I couldn't read. She dropped her head, and I sensed her sadness because of my scolding. It made me feel ashamed.

"I'm sorry, Adolpha. I had no reason to lash out at you like that. I'm afraid my lack of sleep has made me short-tempered."

It was obvious to me at that moment that once one gives the devil an opportunity by committing one sin, he can then easily compound it.

She reached to touch me gently on my arm, but before she could say anything, the bell rang for matins, and we were soon back in the church chanting more psalms. Somehow I made it through all of it—the responsory, the hymn, the versicle, the gospel—without falling asleep. Indeed, by God's grace, the heavy drug of somnolence seemed to have disappeared from my body. I was no longer sleepy, but, God forgive me, I could think of nothing other than the loaves of bread and the bowls of warm milk waiting on the long tables in the refectory.

At last, just before daybreak I was seated at the table dipping chunks of bread in the milk and placing the heavenly morsels in my mouth. As in the courtyard, conversation was not encouraged at table, although it was not completely forbidden. Adolpha, as always, sat next to me, and while we usually managed to exchange a few words, neither of us attempted to speak. Adolpha must have recognized that this time, at least, I preferred to eat. Or else she was still hurt by my unkindness toward her.

Our simple meals were meant to give us the sustenance we needed to serve the Lord as the day wore on. Ordinarily I found they served that purpose well. On that particular morning, however, the warmth of the milk-soaked bread coursed through me like a drug made from the herbs I gathered in the forest. I was in a daze as I walked toward the scriptorium and library, which were a part of the church building. The structure, which abutted the church, was of wood and poor architectural design. The church itself was made of both wood and stone salvaged from ancient Roman monuments, and, while lacking in aesthetics except for the vaulted ceiling, was at least a sturdy structure.

I don't remember walking upstairs to the library. Neither do I know how long I had been sleeping at my desk with my head on my folded arms when Richilda, one of the youngest of the novices, shook me awake.

"Amelia, wake up!" She spoke in a whisper, but there was urgency in that whisper and so much vigor in the manner she shook me that I was momentarily startled. I looked at her, wide-eyed, not knowing for a moment where I was or who she might be. "The king is here," she said.

"The king?"

"King Charles. He's waiting for you. The abbess sent me to find you."

"Oh, oh, of course. The king." I left the codices I'd planned to study on my desk, unopened, and followed young Richilda down the stairs to the scriptorium and out into the courtyard. We walked with haste across the courtyard to Mother Landrada's house.

The man I saw seated across from Mother Landrada in the room she used to receive important visitors was not the king. It's true that he was tall and broad of shoulder, as I'd heard is true of the king, but, by his dress, I knew he was a commoner. What is more, I knew his face, and the sight of it took my breath away. Here sat the man who had materialized out of the mist all those months ago, the same man who had filled my dreams.

He wore a linen shirt and linen breeches and simple hose. The sword he had girt about him suggested that, though he was a commoner, he was a man of some importance, most likely the king's messenger. It gave me a glimmer of hope that he had come bearing the message that His Majesty would not be visiting us after all.

The man was sprawled out in his chair in a relaxed manner, with his long legs extended and crossed at the ankles. By contrast, Mother Landrada, who sat across from him, appeared stiff and ill at ease. The man said something I couldn't quite make out, and followed it with a hearty laugh. He must have sensed that Richilda and I had approached, because he turned his head toward us.

"Ahhh," he said, still smiling and resting his gaze solely upon me. "Are you my little nun?" He spoke in the Francique tongue, and the way he looked at me made my heart pound wildly.

Mother Landrada stood suddenly. "Your Majesty," she said, "I present to you Amalberga of Ardennes, called Amelia, not yet a nun, but she has entered her novitiate."

"Your Majesty," I said, still feeling a little disoriented as I bowed before the big man who was dressed as a commoner.

"Yes," he said, "you are indeed my little nun."

2

MÜNSTER-BILZEN ABBEY

SPRING 794

Amelia

"She is not yet a nun," Mother Landrada repeated, directing her comment to the king. "She has only entered her novitiate."

Her remark embarrassed me, although I'm not certain why. Perhaps it was that I was afraid the king would think me too old to have so recently decided to take the vows, and that I might seem indecisive. Or perhaps it was because I was unused to any remark that focused attention on me. Or could it be I was remembering how it felt to have my arms around him when I was riding behind him on his horse so many months ago? Contrary to anything I expected, however, her words seemed to both please and surprise the king.

"Indeed! You've not yet taken the vows? You're not a

nun?" He smiled at me and spoke as if it were a great thing I'd done by being indecisive.

I dropped my gaze to the floor, not knowing what to say, but wishing with all of my heart I could say or do something that would get us started on the tour of the abbey so we could get it done, and I could get back to my studies. I was quite unaccustomed to the way my body responded to his presence.

"Ah, but she will soon," Mother Landrada said, and I knew she meant it in my defense. "She is quite sincere in her decision after allowing herself plenty of time to make certain it's the will of our Lord. I would entreat Your Majesty to understand that none of the time she's spent here making her decision has been wasted. She is among the most intelligent and well-read of our residents, and everything she does has been oriented toward making herself a better servant of God. And if it please Your Majesty, I would add that she would be a most excellent abbess."

By now my embarrassment was almost unbearable, even though I understood that everything Mother Landrada said was for my benefit and out of her love for me. After all, it is the king who will appoint the next abbess. It is his right to appoint anyone, including any laywoman to whose family he may owe a favor. He has given his own daughters the position of abbess of several monasteries, some holding the office in more than one.

"So you want to govern an abbey, do you?"

I thought his voice sounded amused, as if he were

mocking me, and he was looking at me again, all of which made me blush. This time I refused to cast down my eyes. Instead, I looked at him with as level a gaze as I could manage. It seemed to me that there was something I should say, but the dullness brought on by lack of sleep had returned and rendered me unable to speak. All I could think of was that his eyes were a very interesting blue-gray and that his large nose somehow gave him the appearance of strength.

"Why do you wish to take the veil of a nun?" he asked. "One doesn't have to be under monastic vows to govern an abbey."

"You are most certainly correct, Your Majesty, but I believe one should be."

He raised one of his copper-colored eyebrows. "Oh? And why is that?"

I didn't fail to see the warning look Mother Landrada gave me, but this time, instead of being rendered dumb, I couldn't stop myself from speaking.

"Because, Your Majesty, it is my belief that an abbey should be for holy purposes only, not a means to profit noblemen. Or noblewomen," I added. "Therefore, it should be governed by those whose sole purpose is to serve God."

"Amelia!" Mother Landrada said. "You are speaking in a most improper—"

"Let her speak," the king said, cutting her off. Then, turning back to me, he said, "Your own abbess, the most worthy and efficient Landrada, has taken no vows. Am I to assume you think she is unworthy and, perhaps, incapable as well?"

I saw immediately that I had reaped the unwanted rewards of speaking without thinking. The wisest course would have been not to speak again. Nevertheless, I continued like a braying donkey.

"Mother Landrada is a holy woman, unlike other laypersons who have been granted abbeys. She does not govern the abbey for monetary profit, as some others do. You can see how simple her quarters are," I said, sweeping my hand to indicate the room, bare of anything save a few chairs and a table. There were no carpets on the floor or rich tapestries on the wall. "She does everything out of her devotion to God. None of the profits made from our fields and vineyards go into her coffers. She is, as I said, a holy woman, in spite of the fact that, for her own private reasons, she has never taken the veil." My eyes burned from lack of sleep, and my headache had returned. I wasn't at all certain that what I said made sense.

Mother Landrada was, by now, quite beside herself. "That's enough, Amelia," she said, scowling at me. "His Majesty has no interest in your opinions."

My face once again burned with embarrassment, but, to my surprise, the king came to my defense.

"Of course I have an interest, my dear Landrada. After all, I did ask for her opinion." There was a lightheartedness, almost a chuckle, to his voice as he spoke. "But," he said, turning to me, "we must be done with our talk and get on about the business of inspecting the abbey."

I at least had enough sense this time to indicate my agreement with a bow rather than embarrassing myself by speaking again. Mother Landrada must have been too upset to say a word. She stood as the king stood and made her little bow, but I didn't fail to see the fire in her eyes that was directed at me as I left with the king.

Once we were out of the abbess's quarters, the king took a long, deep breath, as if he were trying to breathe in all of the cool spring air that surrounded us. "Well, Amelia, where shall we start?" he said, looking down at me from his great height.

"Perhaps I should start with an apology, Your Majesty," I said. "I have no doubt that you remember meeting me once before at the edge of the forest. I'm afraid I didn't know who you were and therefore didn't pay you the proper homage. I ask your forgiveness."

"I do indeed remember you," he said, still with that hint of amusement in his voice, "but perhaps I should apologize to you for not telling you at that time who I am."

I was completely taken aback and could think of nothing to say. I'd never even imagined a king seeking my forgiveness. All I could do was stare at him. I saw the amused expression dissolve from his face to be replaced by a puzzled frown.

"I frighten you, Amelia. I wish you wouldn't be."

"I'm not frightened," I said a little too quickly. I was lying, of course, but I didn't want him to think of me as an insecure child. I wanted him to think of me as capable and sensible enough to become abbess of Münster-Bilzen when the time came for the appointment.

"Well, then," he said, "since you're not frightened of me, and since we're now out of the intimidating presence of the abbess, perhaps you will expound further on the appointment of abbots and abbesses. I understand you think I should stop *completely* the practice of distributing monasteries and their governance as rewards to my relatives and my most loyal friends. You just said that the head of a monastery should be a religious, but should they be my appointments, or should the monks and nuns choose their own abbots?"

Again I was stunned that he was continuing to pursue the subject. Beyond that, I was reluctant to answer. If I failed to give him the answer he wanted, he might deny the requests we'd made for repairs at Münster-Bilzen, and, of course, he could eventually deny my future appointment as abbess.

"I . . . I'm afraid I've already said too much on that subject, when I should have said nothing at all, since I'm not capable of making the kind of decisions that kings make."

This time his response was more than slight amusement. He laughed uproariously. "You don't believe that. No more than I do."

"Shall we start with the library?" I said, making a concerted effort to change the subject. My mind was far too dull from lack of sleep to stay in that dangerous quagmire any longer. Besides the fact that I had a particular prejudice for the library, it was the most logical place to start, since it and the church were Mother Landrada's greatest concerns. She sought the king's assistance for repairs to the church and for the acquisition of more books for the library. Our abbey was not, at the present, profitable enough to pay for these things on our own, as some abbeys were. It is true that the abbey, like many others, owned farmland and sold the produce. We also took in some rents and tariffs from the village called Bilzen that had grown up around the core of the monastery. While the abbey was usually rather profitable, our revenues were down because two harsh summers had damaged our crops and therefore our commerce.

"Very well," the king said. "Show me the library."

Mother Landrada's house was only a short distance from the church where the scriptorium, with the library above it, was attached as a sort of annex. In less than a minute we were at the entrance, which, I might add, was no more than a few stone steps leading up to a simple oak door. The scriptorium on the first floor was never particularly crowded, since we had very few manuscripts to copy and only one nun other than me who was capable of copying them in an adequate manner. There were sometimes one or two young novices practicing their writing, as was the case this time. I walked past them, headed for the stairway that led up to the library, but, to my surprise, the king seemed quite interested in the scriptorium, and in particular in the two young women who painstakingly traced letters over and over again in order to perfect their penmanship.

"You link those letters quite well." He leaned over the shoulder of one called Hedwig as he spoke, startling her.

She almost dropped her quill as she jerked her head around to look at him. It was no surprise that she didn't recognize him as the king.

"Sir, you interrupt my work." She spoke with a strained politeness and tried to go back to writing.

I walked toward them as quickly as possible, hoping to avoid a disaster and embarrassment for everyone. "Your Majesty, may I present Hedwig of Austrasia, one of your loyal subjects and one of our newest novices."

It was immediately clear that I had not succeeded in avoiding either disaster or embarrassment. Hedwig's eyes widened and her face went white. In the process of her too-quick climb down from her high stool, she spilled ink on the desk and her habit. She gave a nervous look, then bowed lower than was necessary.

"I had no intention of disturbing you. Please go back to your work." He seemed quite sincere and even helped soak up some of the spilled ink, using the tail of his cloak.

Hedwig was too stunned to move for a moment, until I signaled her with a nod of my head. She picked up her quill, but her hand shook as she tried to trace letters on the ink-blotched paper. Still, King Charles watched her. After a moment he spoke again, still not taking his eyes off the paper.

"It is so difficult," he said, "to know what letter should follow the one before in order to make the string of letters into a word. I practice for hours and still don't have it right."

Young Hedwig looked up from her writing and seemed to be struggling with trying to speak. Mercifully for both of them, the king turned away from her and started for the stairs leading up to the library.

"Perhaps if I had more time . . ." He didn't appear to be speaking to anyone in particular, but musing to himself. "When I am old, perhaps. Then I shall learn to write. When there are no more wars."

When we reached the top of the stairs and the door to the library, he went inside without waiting for me to open the door for him.

"This, Your Majesty, is our poor library," I said, walking behind him. "As you can see, we are in need of more volumes for the education of our residents."

He walked around the room, looking at the sparsely stocked shelves without saying a word and wearing an expression that was impossible to read. At one point he plucked a volume from the shelf and read aloud:

" 'In principio erat Verbum et Verbum erat apud Deum et Deus erat Verbum. Hoc erat in principio apud Deum. Omnia per ipsum facta sunt et sine ipso factum est nihil quod factum est.' "

To which I replied, "Amen."

"Ah, that writing were as easy as reading." He spoke more to himself than to me. He closed the volume. "I see that you have the most important of books," he said.

"I cannot deny that the Holy Bible is the most important of books, but in order to enrich one's understanding, one needs to be well-read in other matters as well," I said, fearing that his words meant he would not be inclined to grant us funds for the library.

"Other matters?" he asked. "Such as . . . ?"

"Oh, all things, Your Majesty. Arithmetic, agriculture, architecture, astrology, poetry, the works of Virgil and Homer—"

"Are you saying, Amelia, that one must be learned to understand God's will and achieve salvation? Are you saying that the poor peasant who cannot read at all will be condemned to the fires of hell simply because of his ignorance?" He had brought himself closer to me by a few steps and looked down at me from his great height in a manner that he must have meant to be intimidating.

"Certainly not," I said, willing my voice not to tremble and forcing myself to look up directly into his eyes. "God shares his bountiful love and salvation with all who seek him. But when my own mind and soul are enriched by reading and educating myself, I feel closer to God. Also, I am sure Your Majesty understands the importance of preserving knowledge, since I have heard your own library is substantial. In order to preserve that knowledge properly, one must be versed in it."

"So," he said, still looking down at me, "you have found that reading the works of pagan poets and sages is necessary for your own salvation."

"Begging your pardon, Your Majesty, but that is not at all what I said or what I meant. I know that my salvation comes through the grace of God through our Lord Jesus Christ. But the preservation of knowledge does not mean—"

"I shall have to give this rather pagan idea of yours some

thought," he said, turning away from me and giving the room and its sparsely stocked shelves another look.

My heart seemed to stop, and my mouth went dry. I had succeeded not in convincing him of our great need, but in making him believe I was a pagan.

"And now we will look at the church," he said as he started for the stairs. I had no choice but to follow, but not before I gave a longing glance toward the high desk where I had left my books.

As we entered the courtyard that surrounds the building, I could see that the morning sun had come out to dance on the budding leaves of the trees and had kissed the air with a promise of warmth. The king seemed to revel in the promise, and once again he breathed deeply of the air, which was already faintly scented with spring's first brave flowers. I could do no more than dally there with him, while I wanted nothing other than to hurry along and get the ordeal over and done.

At last he picked up his pace and walked toward the door to the church. He commanded me to walk beside him when I tried to observe the proper protocol and remain slightly behind. "It's such a nuisance to have to keep turning around to speak to you," he said.

As I have noted before, the church was made of both wood and stone, with the walls being a rough-cut stone. I have also mentioned that the church was not particularly grand or beautiful, except for the high vaulted wooden ceiling, and of course the spiritual beauty that is always imparted by the presence of the Host.

King Charles dipped his hand in the basin of holy water as we entered, crossed himself, and walked to the front, where he knelt in prayer. I, of course, was obliged to follow his lead. He prayed for a very long time, and I felt myself once again drifting into sleep. I was startled awake by his rather loud "Amen" and rose to follow him out of the church. We were almost out when I suddenly remembered that I was obliged to mention to him that the roof needed repair and to point out the rotting beams and the place where the water had run down the southernmost wall, doing considerable damage to a wooden statue of Saint Michael the Archangel. All I could do now was mention the needed repairs without pointing them out, which I did as quickly as possible.

We went to the refectory next, which, though it is unbearably cold in winter and stifling hot in summer and is furnished with only the crudest of wooden tables, at least is not in need of repair, so that we had no need to linger. I was also obliged to show him the bakery and brewery, both of which Mother Landrada insisted were too small. Once I pointed out the size, I felt there was nothing more to say, so we moved on. I was thankful that the king asked very few questions to slow me down. We were on our way to the infirmary, where I was supposed to point out that the room for bleeding and purgation needed considerable repair. It was to be the last stop on the tour. The king stopped before we were halfway there.

"You are in a considerable hurry, Amelia," he said, turning to me.

"It is only that I am trying not to waste Your Majesty's time," I said. At least that is what I think I said. I had begun to feel as if my mind were filling with cobwebs, leaving no room for thoughts to form properly. It was an effort for me to make my tongue behave enough to form words, and my eyes ached for want of sleep.

He looked at me for several seconds, not saying a word. I couldn't decipher his thoughts, nor imagine why he wore that slight smile. A memory came to me once again unbidden, of how it had felt to have my arms about him and to have his warmth against me as I rode behind him. It was something I thought I had forgotten, and which, now that it kept resurfacing today, both surprised and confused me. For one impossible moment as our eyes held, I had the irrational feeling that he was remembering the same thing. I forced myself to avert my eyes, breaking the spell.

"The infirmary is this way," I said, pointing.

When we reached the building, I once again opened the door for him, and he stepped inside.

"The building is small, with room for no more than two patients, and difficult to keep clean because of the crowded working conditions." I was aware that my voice was flat and that I sounded uninterested. I pointed to the bloodstained floor just as I had been instructed to do and hoped he wouldn't want to stay long, since the very thought of bleeding and purgation were unpleasant to me.

"Yes," he said, looking at the floor and the equally bloodstained walls. "I can see that it is small. I saw, too, that your church ceiling leaks and your library is inadequate, and I can see that you would rather be doing anything other than escorting your king."

"Oh, no, no!" I stammered. "Not at all, Your Majesty. It is my honor to—"

"I suspect you'd rather be at your books, and that is commendable," he said, continuing to inspect the room. "You are right to educate yourself if you want to be abbess." He turned to me and said in a deceptively pleasant tone, "However, if you really want to govern a monastery, you must learn to be shrewd and cunning. Especially when you're dealing with the king."

3

The Palace at Aix-la-Chapelle
Spring 794

Charles

The king was alone in the great bathing pool he'd had built east of the palace and enclosed with a magnificent stone structure. It was unusual for him to swim alone. There were times when he had up to a hundred of his officers and assistants in the pool with him, and more in the six pools housed in other rooms of the bathhouse. Now, however, he wanted to be alone. He needed time to think. But to think properly, he had to get the young Amelia out of his mind. The first time he'd seen her that day in the mist he'd been entranced by her ethereal beauty and had even fancied her to be one of the goddesses of the forest the Saxons talked about. He'd never guessed he'd meet her again, and certainly would never have guessed her to be so intelligent, or that she would invade his mind the way she had done the last two days.

He'd thought some time in the baths would clear his mind. The bathhouse had been rebuilt by Pepin the Elder, Charles's father, more than thirty years ago from the ruins of old spring-fed Roman baths. The pagan idols had been removed, the pools repaired and enlarged, and a new structure built around them.

His powerful arms propelled him through the water with slow, rhythmical strokes. He swam without stopping for an hour, as was his habit daily when he was at Aix, since the water was always a pleasant temperature summer and winter.

As he swam, he forced himself to try to solve the problem that nagged at him. There was clear evidence that his son, Pepin, known as the Hunchback, had plotted against him in his recent absence while he battled the Huns along the Danube. Pepin, it seemed, had made a pact with several magnates to overthrow their king and put himself on the throne. It could not be done, of course. None of them had the cunning to execute such a coup, nor the leadership ability to keep a kingdom intact. Although with more maturity Pepin might one day have made a good king.

Now the truth of their betrayal was out, and the magnates, all Franks whom he'd considered loyal, were locked in a dungeon, while Pepin was confined to his quarters under heavy guard. The magnates would be executed, or perhaps—in the case of Radbertis and Lothair, who were less culpable—simply have their eyes gouged out. But what of Pepin? Pepin, his eldest son, whom he cherished, whose childish poems written in the palace school he still kept, whose mother, a concubine, was his first love. He remembered still the day the boy was born, the pride he felt, the love. He'd grown into a handsome boy, but some strange illness had struck him in his early years, drawing him over in pain and leaving his back misshapen. The deformity had not lessened Charles's love for the boy.

Pepin was a man now, no more than five years away from thirty. He would have to be punished. By all that was right and just, he deserved death. But how could Charles kill his own son, who had come from his own loins?

The visit a few days earlier to the abbey at Münster-Bilzen had given him an excuse to leave the palace, and the long ride gave him a chance to think. He had done just that—thought and puzzled over what to do about Pepin during the ride to and from the abbey. But he had come to no decision.

Today he had swum fifty laps in the enormous pool, trying to decide his course of action. He knew it wouldn't do to discuss the problem with Fastrada, his wife. She had never liked Pepin and had treated him with a cruelty Charles could never understand. Perhaps it was because she had borne him only daughters and was exhibiting her jealousy that Pepin might someday rule the Frankish kingdom. Perhaps it was something else. Something womanish that no man could fathom.

As Charles hefted himself out of the water, he accepted a robe from one of his servants, wrapped it around his naked body, and walked, still distracted, toward the palace. He'd not gone half the distance when he heard a voice calling him from behind and recognized it immediately as Einhard's.

"Your Majesty! Your Majesty, a word with you, please."

Charles turned around to see the young man, small of stature and stocky, always in a hurry and possessed of inexhaustible energy. Einhard hurried toward him carrying a stack of documents.

"Yes, my young friend," Charles said, waiting for him. "What is it that has you in such a rush?"

"The seneschal has asked me to give you these documents, Your Majesty," Einhard said, still hurrying toward him. "They are an inventory of the royal fiscs you requested so you can estimate your revenues."

Charles looked down at the little man who always seemed to be in motion. He was young, perhaps the same age as his oldest surviving daughter, Bertha. Perhaps the same age as Amelia, the would-be nun who still invaded his thoughts.

"Thank you, Einhard," he said, taking the stack of documents from the young man. He'd brought Einhard into his court two years ago on the advice of Alcuin, who was the head of the court school. Einhard had received his education there and proven to be as intelligent and capable as Alcuin promised he would be. Einhard was an important addition to the palace school, as well as to the court. He not only served as a teacher when Alcuin was absent, but he'd also proven himself capable of diplomatic endeavors. Charles had sent him on several such missions.

Einhard made his bow to the king and was already bustling away when Charles called him back.

"Einhard! A word with you!"

The young man stopped, whirled around, and hurried back to the king's side almost in one movement. "Yes, my lord," he said, bowing again.

"Join me for my breakfast, Einhard. There is something I would discuss with you."

"I'm at your service, Father." Einhard was slightly breathless as he took two steps to Charles's one long stride. The young man often referred to him as Father, and there were times when Charles wished he were his true flesh and blood. He loved his own four sons and admired the unique talents of each, but he couldn't converse with any of them on the same level as he was able to talk with Einhard. In spite of his outward show of nervous energy, Einhard's mind ran in an ordered, analytical, and perceptive way that few could rival.

They walked across an expanse of grass along a path leading from the baths to the square and a compound of buildings, past the church to a house with a great porch that was the entrance to the palace. Charles's private chamber was on the first floor of the residential building, and it was here that he led Einhard.

The outer room was decorated with paintings of heroes from ancient times, as well as some of Charles himself. Charles cared little for the paintings, since, to his mind, they were far too unrealistic. The figures depicting humans and animals were stiff, often with heads too large and limbs too long or too short, and they, as well as buildings, seemed stacked on top of one another with no perspective of distance. He much preferred the images he could conjure in his imagination when he read or listened to poetry.

The outer room of his chambers was cold, as it often was on early mornings in spring. As soon as they entered, Einhard rushed toward the crackling fervor of the hearth at the north end of the room.

"Wait here, friend, until I am dressed," Charles said, smiling to himself at the young man's eagerness for the fire. "I'll have a cup of mulled wine sent out to warm you."

Charles rubbed his flesh dry with the robe he'd worn from the baths, then dressed in the simple linen shirt and breeches he usually wore in preference to cumbersome royal robes. His personal servant made no attempt to help him, knowing the king preferred to dress without assistance. When he emerged from his bedchamber, Einhard was huddled close to the fire, sipping his wine. He stood as soon as he saw the king, bowed, and remained standing until Charles was seated and motioned with his hand for him to resume his seat.

"I trust the wine is to your satisfaction," Charles said as he picked up his own cup.

"It is indeed, Your Majesty." Einhard settled back into his chair. One of the things Charles admired about the young man was that, in spite of his perpetual motion when he was about his duties, he never showed even veiled signs of impatience with the king. No matter how curious he might be about why the king had summoned him, he waited with uncompromised forbearance.

Because of that, Charles would respect him and get immediately to the point.

"I want to talk to you about Pepin," he said.

"Pepin." He said the name not as a surprised question, but as matter of course. And still he waited with impeccable patience.

"He must be punished for his rebellion and his betrayal." Charles forced his voice to remain strong and even in spite of the heartbreak he felt.

"Yes . . ." Einhard said. It was impossible to tell whether his remark was agreement or merely encouragement for the king to continue.

"As you must know, I am loath to have him put to death or his body mutilated. He is my son, and no matter what his offense, I hold him dear to my heart. Yet, for his own sake and for the sake of the kingdom, there must be some consequence to his action."

Einhard didn't speak for a long time. Charles was aware of him looking into his eyes, studying his face.

"This," he said finally, setting his cup of wine aside, "is something that should not be settled by any of us who are nothing more than members of the court or of your council, no matter how honorable and prestigious those positions may be."

For the first time, Charles felt a stirring of irritation. "I wouldn't have asked your advice had I not thought you worthy of considering the matter."

"Certainly I understand that, Your Majesty." Einhard didn't flinch or drop his eyes at the king's chastisement. "My advice to you as a confidant is that you cannot take his life or mutilate his body, because your own soul will not tolerate it. Yet, I would tell you, he deserves punishment for his own sake and for the sake of the kingdom. In a word, I can do no more than agree with you. As for the final decision, because it is a matter of the heart, I am both flattered and frightened that you've asked my advice."

"Get on with it, Einhard." Charles made no attempt to hide his irritation.

"Imprison him, Your Majesty. For the rest of his life."

"Imprison him . . ." Charles murmured the words to no one in particular, running his fingers through the curls of his short, rust-colored beard as he mused, only vaguely aware that Einhard was still with him until the young man spoke again.

"It's a heavy burden you bear, Father. No one would envy you. Perhaps the queen—"

"Consulting the queen is out of the question," Charles said, cutting him off. "I'm afraid she's part of the reason Pepin came to do what he did." Charles glanced at the young man who sat silently waiting. Einhard would never push his king for more details or ask him what he meant. "She can be cruel," Charles continued, knowing that of all his confidants, Einhard was the most discreet. "She was most certainly pitiless to my poor misshapen son. But you know that, of course. You know she saw him as unworthy of inheriting the kingdom. I think it especially galled her because she produced no son to rival him or my other sons. Only daughters." Charles looked away, staring at the fire, as if he might find the answer he sought in the dance of the flames. "Perhaps it was my fault as well for indulging Fastrada, or at least not chastising her for her cruelty."

Charles knew he could plead that he was too busy to deal with a trivial matter like a woman's cruelty and jealousy. He could say he was occupied with too many wars, too many treaties, too many soldiers to garrison and feed, too many subjects to see after. A less intelligent man than Einhard would have offered that very defense on the king's behalf. But Einhard kept quiet, perhaps because he knew it was a weak defense. A man should find the time to set things right with his family. Or perhaps the wise Einhard knew that by his silence, Charles's self-blame would be more potent. Charles was lost in his own thoughts for several seconds, remembering Pepin's mother, a concubine he'd sent away, remembering the late Queen Hildegard, whom he had honored and respected above all his wives, and who had given him three fine sons besides his daughters. Would that she were here to advise him now, he thought. But there was no use dwelling on what could not be. He glanced up at Einhard, who still waited in silence.

"Well, Einhard, since neither of us can solve the problem immediately, what say you to breakfast?" Charles said, standing.

Einhard sprang to his feet. "It would be my honor to break my fast in your company, Your Majesty."

Charles gave the young man a hearty clap on the back. "Ah, my good fellow, you always know the correct thing to say." He threw his arm over Einhard's stocky shoulders and led him toward the dining room.

The king's dining room was as long, dark, and cold as a cave, and the oak table was stained with wine and grease and other spills from royal feasts. The roasted joint of venison—brown, sizzling, and seeping a fine scent along with its juices—sat on a wooden trencher at one end of the table. Around it were steaming bowls of porridge and lentils, as well as a loaf of bread and a flask of wine with a tall cup. Before the two men were seated, a servant appeared with another cup and disappeared just as quickly.

Charles reached one of his large hands toward the meat, tore off a succulent piece, and handed it, steaming and dripping, to Einhard, then tore a similar chunk for himself.

"Eat," he said to the young man when he saw him hesitate.

"It's roast venison, Your Majesty," Einhard said, still hesitating.

"Indeed it is," Charles said, speaking around the mouthful he was chewing. With his free hand, he tipped the wine flask and filled both cups.

"But, Your Majesty, I thought the doctors—"

"Doctors be damned," Charles said. He tore off a piece of the bread and dipped it first into the lentils and then into the porridge before placing it in his mouth. "I know the doctors tell me roast meat is bad for my body," he said when he had swallowed the bread. "They tell me to eat boiled meat. Have you ever eaten boiled meat, Einhard?"

"I have, Your Majesty. Once when you sent me to the island kingdoms of the Britons on a diplomatic mission."

"And what say you of their boiled meat?"

"It would be more pleasant to die young of too much roast venison than to live a long life eating boiled meat."

Charles laughed, sloshing the wine from his cup as he raised it to Einhard. "You are very wise, my man. Here," he said, ripping off another piece of the venison and handing it to Einhard. "And here's to short but happy lives void of boiled meat."

The toast brought a smile to Einhard's face and a twinkle to his eyes. He tore at the meat with his teeth and followed it with a swallow of wine. It wasn't until Charles had filled his cup twice that the young scholar leaned forward and addressed the king without having been spoken to first.

"Just wanted you to know, Your Majesty, that when I mentioned the queen earlier, I wasn't going to suggest you consult her. I was only going to say the same thing you voiced—that perhaps the queen had been partly to blame for Pepin's actions, since the two are not compatible."

Charles made no reply. He was thinking that Einhard, besides being scholarly, also had a clear mind with a practical streak. Perhaps, he thought, he should use him even more frequently for diplomatic missions. The ones he'd sent him on so far had been those of relatively small importance.

"I beg your forgiveness, Your Majesty," Einhard said, mistaking the king's silence for a sign of disapproval. "I fear I have spoken out of turn regarding the queen. I have exceeded the bounds of propriety by suggesting she has been in any way at fault. A man like me should never speak when he drinks wine and should never drink wine when he speaks."

"You are quite observant of mankind," Charles said, leaving Einhard to wonder whether it was his recognizing the queen's faults or his own that compelled the king to call him observant.

"If I have failed you in my advice, may I suggest that one of your daughters might be of better use in helping you decide Pepin's fate. It's my belief that a woman's tender heart, while it renders her useless in many ways, can be of some worth when a decision must be tempered with mercy."

"Do you really believe," Charles said, sopping up the last of the lentils with his bread, "that a woman's advice can be useful?"

"At times, Your Majesty. Under certain circumstances. If the situation is not overly complex. It may please you to remember that your second wife, the late Hildegard, could be quite helpful and occasionally even wise."

"Indeed," Charles said, musing, remembering again Hildegard's strength and wisdom. Fastrada, his current wife, was also quick of mind and capable, but she lacked tenderness, to use Einhard's word, to make her truly effective. He considered for a moment Einhard's suggestion that he consult one of his daughters, but quickly dismissed it. Hruodrud and Bertha were too preoccupied with their own lives and children and with the abbeys they expected to receive. Gisela was too sickly. Theoderada could think of nothing at the moment save her lovers, and Hiltrud and Ruodhaid were too young.

Perhaps he'd been wrong to forbid his daughters to marry. Perhaps a son-in-law would be helpful now. He quickly dismissed that thought as well. He didn't want to complicate his life with sons-in-law vying for his throne. Anyway, his daughters seemed content to satisfy themselves with lovers and with the children they produced with them. But Einhard was right—there were some things best discussed with a woman.

Charles picked up his wineglass, studying the young man across from him. "Einhard, my good friend," he said, leaning back in his chair. "I believe I have another mission for you."

The young man looked up. "I'm at your service, Your Majesty." His expression was eager, excited.

"This may prove to be difficult and may take your best diplomatic skills."

"I'm flattered and pleased you think I'm capable of a difficult mission, Father. Where would you have me go?"

"To Münster-Bilzen."

"The abbey?" Einhard's expression was both confused and a bit crestfallen.

"There's someone there I want you to bring to the palace. A young woman. Soon to be a nun, I believe."

4

MÜNSTER-BILZEN ABBEY

SPRING 794

Amelia

It was just after sext, and I was in the hops fields along with Ambrose, who was the abbey's steward. Mother Landrada had granted me permission to oversee the marling of the soil. I'd had a great deal of difficulty convincing Ambrose to do the marling.

His justification for his reluctance was simply that marling had never been done in the past, while I suspect the real reason was that he didn't want to go to the trouble of hauling in the silt and river soil that would enrich the land. I'd heard about the technique from a traveler from the northern islands who stayed in the abbey for a short time. He said it would help heal the exhaustion the soil suffers from planting it year after year. The stranger also taught me about the technique of manuring the soil, but so far I'd used that technique only on the vegetable garden. I was pleased with the results and planned to use it in the fields as well.

Since Mother Landrada had herself granted me permission to be in the fields that day, I was greatly surprised when young Richilda once again approached me with a summons from the abbess.

"Are you certain I am the one she sent for? Could it be you misunderstood the name?" I knew I sounded annoyed, which made Richilda appear timid.

"I . . . I'm sorry to disturb you, my sister, but I am quite sure it is you she asked for. She even told me where I would find you."

My annoyance only intensified, and I had to close my eyes and send up a quick prayer for tranquillity before I answered her. "Very well," I said, throwing down the wooden rake I'd been using to demonstrate to Ambrose the technique I wanted him to use. It was obvious by the testy sound of my voice that my prayer had not been answered. "Ambrose, continue with the work. I shall be back shortly to see that it's done right," I called over my shoulder as I glanced at Richilda, who by now was cowering. "What does she want with me?" I asked. That only made her cower more.

She mumbled something incomprehensible that I surmised meant she didn't know. As we walked back toward the walls of the abbey, I sent up another silent prayer for help to overcome my feelings of resentment. It might not have been so difficult to accomplish except that Mother Landrada had, of late, begun to send one of the young novitiates to fetch me more and more often, and usually when I was in the middle of something important.

Her health had made no improvement in spite of the frequent bleedings she received. In fact, she'd grown weaker, and her breathing was considerably more labored. Because of that she relied heavily on the other nuns and novices, especially Adolpha and me, to help her carry out her duties.

"It matters little to me that you are a novice," she said. "You and Adolpha are the wisest of my daughters, and God has given you to me to rely upon."

And so we were called frequently, sometimes to help her with her accounts, sometimes because she wanted to discuss what to do about the miller, who, she suspected, was stealing grain, but whose wife and children would starve if she sent him away. Sometimes she only wanted help moving a table or a chest. More and more I'd come to suspect that she fabricated excuses to send for us because the thought of her impending death made her seek comfort in the presence of another human.

As Richilda and I approached Mother Landrada's residence, I could see through the open door that she had company. A young man was with her. He was short but broad of shoulder, with worry lines just beginning to be etched in the space between his eyes. The last time she had called me when she had a guest, it had been the king. However, unlike the king, this young man stood as soon as I entered.

"You are Amalberga of the Ardennes, called Amelia?" His eyes inspected me from head to toe.

I gave Mother Landrada a quick questioning glance, but I could read little from her face. "I am," I said.

"I am here to take you to the king."

I was so taken aback I couldn't speak, and when I looked at Mother Landrada again, her face was expressionless. "The king?" I sounded as if I were dull-witted.

"He wishes to consult with you," he said.

I shook my head. "But I am neither worthy nor wise enough to be—"

"Sit down, please, Amelia." Mother Landrada's voice sounded weary.

I sat, but I was tense and on the edge of my chair. I will admit that I had entertained thoughts of seeing the king again, but I had no wish to be taken away from the abbey. Especially not now, when the fields were being planted and I still had so much studying to do. Mother Landrada spoke again.

"Amelia, this is Einhard, a scholar from the court of King Charles. He has brought us the good news that the king may be inclined to look favorably upon our request for aid to the abbey."

Of course, I knew immediately what those words really meant: I was being used as a bargaining chip. The abbey's needs would be met if I would go to the king. But what did it mean that he said he wished to consult with me? He seemed to disagree with everything I'd said when I saw him before, so I couldn't imagine why he would want to ask me anything. I felt a sudden void in my chest when I realized there could be another reason. King Charles was known to be very fond of women. He'd sent one of his wives away because she didn't please him, and I'd heard he'd sent concubines away as well. Could it be he would bring me to his court for immoral purposes? It was widely known that many nuns had lovers whom they visited from time to time, but surely the king didn't think I was such a woman. And even if he did, how could Mother Landrada ask me to do it?

I looked at her again and saw her resigned smile. "It's all right, Amelia." Her voice was soft. "You can come back when your duty to the king is done."

What did that mean? I wondered. What did she assume my duty to the king would be? I felt as if I might cry, thinking that she would throw me out to such a destiny. But when I looked at her face, I saw nothing save her loving smile.

"I am certain you both know that the king is an honorable man." Einhard's words caught me by surprise, and I turned my glance away from Mother Landrada to look at him. "His Majesty will make certain, my dear abbess, that your daughter is treated with kindness and respect and that she is returned to you in good health."

It was as if this Einhard had read my thoughts, for I knew that there was another meaning behind those words *good health*.

"Of course," Mother Landrada said, as if she had never expected anything else.

"How long must I be gone?" I was angry that I was being asked to leave the abbey at such a crucial time, and I was quite certain the anger could be heard in my voice.

"His Majesty didn't tell me how long he will need your counsel, miss, but I ask you to bear in mind that the distance from here to the palace at Aix-la-Chapelle requires at least two days' journey by horse, even in the best of circumstances."

Two days there and two days back. Even if I was asked to stay only two days, that would be almost a week away from my work. Besides, I had no horse to ride.

"His Majesty speaks highly of you, Miss Amelia," Einhard said, and I could see the intelligence in his eyes. "He says you have a good mind. He has honored you by asking you to advise him, and it is, of course, the duty of all of his subjects to serve him."

"My first duty is to God," I said, still not able to dissolve my anger, in spite of all the reassurance Einhard had given.

"Certainly," Einhard said with a white-hot wit burning in his eyes, "and there is no conflict in serving God and the king."

I could only stare at him, thinking he had no idea of what conflicts I might feel. Finally Mother Landrada spoke, breaking a silence that threatened to shatter from its own weight.

"You are free to leave now, Amelia. You may go back to your work, or, if you prefer, you may prepare for the journey. Master Einhard has brought a horse for you to ride. He will stay the night in our guest quarters and wishes to leave early tomorrow at lauds. You have permission to be absent at matins."

I replied, "Yes, Mother," there being nothing else possible

to say, and left after a little bow in her direction but not even a nod to the man called Einhard.

I went back to the fields and worked beside Ambrose, who was nursing his own anger, until it was time for vespers. When the prayers were over, I walked with Adolpha to the refectory.

"What did the king's man want with you?" she asked as soon as we were out of the church.

"Word spreads fast, I see."

"But not details," Adolpha said. "What did he want?"

"Shhh," I said, because we were too close to another cluster of nuns. I managed to avoid answering her until we were seated in the refectory with the psalms sung and the prayers repeated. We were just being served our supper of more bread soaked in milk when she nudged me.

"You can tell me now. What did that man want?" She spoke in a whisper and without looking at me.

"I have to leave the abbey for a while," I said, answering her in the same manner.

Adolpha almost dropped her cup, and a little of the milk sloshed out onto the table. "You're being sent away?"

I gave her a sideways glance and saw that her face was almost as pale as the milk. "So it seems."

"With him?" she asked, still whispering.

I nodded, looking into the well of my cup.

She touched my arm surreptitiously—a signal of compassion. "It doesn't matter what you've done; I shall always love you as my dearest sister. And I shall pray for you. Without ceasing."

I turned toward her when I realized she assumed something dreadful, something other than the truth.

"It's not what you think," I said. "Mother Landrada is sending me away because the king has commanded me to come to his court."

I spoke the last a little too loudly, and every head at the table turned to look at me. The eyes of the nun who sat across from me widened, and I could see an irreverent curiosity swimming in the deep blue pools.

"The king? Commanded you to his court?" the nun, whose name was Gertrude, asked.

"Shhh! We shouldn't be speaking of this now," I said, once again looking into the depths of my cup. No one spoke after that, but I could feel the nettles of their curiosity pricking the silence. Later, after we walked out of the refectory with the solemnity Saint Benedict required, a frenzied flock of my sisters in Christ crowded around me, pestering me to feed them my story.

"What does the king want with you?" "Will you go?" "For how long?" "Are you being punished?" "Will you bring us honor?" "Dishonor?" "Are you frightened?" "Why would he want you?"

The questions swirled around me in such a manner that I felt as if I were being pecked to death by noisy crows. I kept trying to speak, but it was impossible. Finally Adolpha quieted them in her commanding way with only the slightest raising of her voice.

"The king has summoned her, and Mother has bid her

go. That's all you have need of knowing. When she returns, I am certain she will give us a full accounting."

The nuns grew quiet, except for one, who after a moment said, "We should know if it is the devil's bidding she does."

Adolpha came to my defense quickly. "Evil thoughts enter your mind, Sister. You should purge yourself of—"

Before she could finish, I interrupted her, taking up my own sword. "The king's messenger has told me only that His Majesty wishes to consult with me on a matter regarding his family." Just as one of them started to interrupt, I added, "I know not what the matter concerns, and I know not why he thinks I could be of any help to him. I know only that Mother has bid me go. And Adolpha is correct: I will give you a full accounting as soon as I can."

I was not certain that my words would still them, but Adolpha immediately reminded them in her stern voice that the prayers of compline would begin in a few minutes.

"Thank you, Adolpha," I whispered. She smiled and touched my arm again. I could feel her love and concern for me, but I also sensed her own curiosity, a hot wind pushing at me in silence.

After compline, we were expected to return to our cells and go to bed in order to be sufficiently rested for prayers at three a.m., so I had no opportunity to speak to Adolpha again that night. Neither did I speak to her or even see her the next morning before I left the abbey, riding the mare Einhard brought for me. We left the gate side by side, he on a mare also.

We rode for several hours on that cold spring morning with neither of us speaking, although I was filled with questions I wanted to ask but was not certain of the propriety of it. Einhard kept pushing the mare he rode to walk faster and faster until she was almost in a trot, and I had to urge my own mount with little kicks to her ribs to keep up. Eventually I grew concerned that we would tire the mares too quickly, and I told Einhard as much.

He glanced back over his shoulder when I spoke to him. He didn't reply, but he did, at least, slow a little. Before long he picked up the gait again, and once again I called out to him.

"Forgive me, Einhard, but I must ask you once more to slow the pace. See how the mares are sweating even in this cool air? I fear you'll give them a distemper."

This time he didn't glance back at me, but he pulled back on the reins, slowing his mount. From my position behind him, I could see how his shoulders tensed and how he seemed to have difficulty sitting still, which I knew must have tired his mare even more. I concluded that he was either possessed of a highly nervous temperament, or else there was some great crisis at the palace that needed the attention of both of us. No matter what his reason for being so agitated, it didn't change the fact that he was pushing the horses too hard and that my bladder felt in need of emptying. Also, my stomach felt hollow and wanted to be filled with the bread and cheese Mother Landrada had sent along with us.

I called out once again to his back, "Einhard! I have need of a rest."

He turned around to look at me, and when he saw that I had pulled my mare to a stop, he became even more agitated.

"A rest? Oh! Oh, yes, of course." He rode toward me ridiculously fast and stopped in front of me. "I . . . I should have thought of . . . It's just that I'm not accustomed to being in the company of wo . . . Certainly you have your needs. Certainly . . ." Besides stammering, he was as breathless as if he himself had been trotting along at a fast pace.

"Perhaps we should have a repast," I said.

"What? Oh, yes! Yes, of course." He scrambled off of his mare and walked at a rapid pace toward an outcropping of rocks, reminding me of a little mouse scurrying around the granary.

I slipped away behind some of the rocks to relieve my aching bladder, and when I returned, Einhard seemed even more ill at ease. However, he did consent to sit on one of the boulders and join me as we ate the bread and cheese and sipped from the wineskin we'd brought from the abbey.

"Tell me, if you will, what is the nature of the problem regarding the king's family," I said finally, hoping a little conversation would put him at ease.

"I'm afraid I'm not at liberty to discuss the king's business," he said.

After another long silence, I asked, "Are you one of the king's scholars?" I knew that he was, for Mother Landrada had told me as much. I was still trying to put him at ease with conversation.

"*Scholar* is a title I don't deserve. I have much to learn."

"As do I," I said. "For example, I have not yet solved the Diophantus puzzle."

"Ah, yes, the puzzle," he said, and for the first time I saw him smile. "The age of Diophantus at his death was—"

"Is it his age that is important?" I said, seeing immediately how annoyed he was that I had interrupted him. "Isn't the greater puzzle how life can be so fragile and loss so tragic?"

"Indeed," he said, "but one can see the moral lesson you refer to in the numbers. For example, 'God granted Diophantus to be a boy for the sixth part of his life, and adding a twelfth part to this, he clothed his cheeks with down. He lit him the light of wedlock after a seventh part, and five years after his marriage he granted him a son. Alas! Late-born wretched child; after attaining the measure of half his father's life, chill Fate took him. After consoling his grief by this science of numbers for four years, he ended his life.' "

And so he went on, quoting this and other ancient riddles and explaining a man's life and his grief to me with mathematics. It settled his nerves. Except, of course, when I disagreed with him, which I did sometimes for my own amusement.

5

Aix-la-Chapelle

Spring 794

Charles

The chair Charles occupied in the great hall of his private apartments was not his official throne, but it had been placed on a platform while those with whom he conferred were seated at a table below him.

The raised position, along with his superior height, gave him the advantage of being able to see the courtyard from the window in the stone wall to his right. It enabled him also to see Einhard and the girl ride into the palace grounds. Their arrival momentarily distracted him from the Bulgar chieftain, who, along with his cohorts, had come to propose an alliance against the caliph of Baghdad.

While Adalgisus, the court chamberlain, conferred with the chieftain and his counselors, Charles watched Einhard help Amelia dismount. Einhard seemed even more agitated than usual. He was hopping from one foot to the other, and he didn't seem to know what to do with his hands. When Amelia was dismounted and standing, Einhard fidgeted in such an awkward fashion that he might have been mistaken for a half-wit. He attempted a bow to the girl, and his cap slid down his face, dangling for a moment on his nose when he quickly straightened. When the cap fell to the ground, Einhard bent over in an attempt to retrieve it but in the process bumped his head against Amelia's knee.

Charles had to place a hand over his mouth to stifle a laugh. It appeared Einhard was smitten with the girl.

"Is something wrong, Your Majesty?"

The long silence that followed the question brought Charles back to the meeting he was supposed to be having with the Bulgarians just as Amelia retrieved the cap for Einhard with a quick and youthful grace.

"Your Majesty?" the chamberlain said again. A worried frown rippled his face.

"Proceed," Charles said with as much royal dignity as he could muster.

"Besides the fifty head each of cattle and sheep the chieftain brought with him, he has just offered an additional fifty head in exchange for your protection," Adalgisus said, translating. "Shall I tell him you accept?"

"Tell him I want an additional hundred head of each." As Charles spoke, he made a concerted effort not to turn his attention back to the courtyard. He waited while his chamberlain translated his counteroffer, and waited even longer while the chieftain grumbled something, then turned to his lieutenant to confer. He seemed to be taking an extraordinarily long time. Charles was about to tell Adalgisus that he would settle for an additional seventy-five each just to get the negotiations over with so he could welcome Amelia properly. He had not been particularly impressed with the Bulgar's livestock anyway. His greatest advantage in the deal would be that he would gain the fierce Bulgar tribesmen as soldiers against the caliph.

"The royal chieftain accepts your offer," Adalgisus said before Charles could concede.

"Excellent!" Charles said. "Tell him I expect delivery before the end of summer."

It took several more minutes of negotiations and complaints by the chieftain that it would take more than a few months to drive livestock such a distance. Finally an agreement was reached. The chieftain stood and bowed to Charles without erasing an angry frown from his face. Regardless of his anger over the hard bargain, Charles knew the livestock would be forthcoming, and he'd have a valuable ally.

"Tell Einhard I wish to see him," Charles said as the Bulgar entourage left. He made the command when they were barely out of the room and before Adalgisus could gush his praises about what a wise bargain the king had made. Charles detested the chamberlain's brand of overly enthusiastic praise, and the truth was, there was nothing to honor anyway. Charles knew he could have demanded an even better bargain had he not been in such a hurry to see Amelia.

He'd never before sacrificed his shrewdness or shirked his duties for a woman. It wasn't a habit he wanted to create. This time had been different, though, because he'd never before seen a woman who wasn't eager to be in his company and to please him.

Einhard arrived, looking tired and slightly disheveled. There was evidence he had attempted to comb his hair, but he left a tuft sticking up at the crown of his head. He'd also tried to wash his face, but there was a streak of dirt on the left side.

"The journey was difficult?" Charles asked, motioning for Einhard to sit across from him.

"The weather was fair and the road no more treacherous than usual, my lord."

"Nevertheless, you look a little worse for the wear, Einhard. Something must have rendered the journey difficult."

Einhard shifted his broad shoulders, looking uncomfortable. "It was the woman, Your Majesty."

"The woman?" Charles said, pretending surprise. "She was unruly?"

"Not that, my lord."

"Sickly?"

"Not that I know of."

"Well, then, difficult in what way?" Charles asked.

"It is simply that she disturbed my . . ."

"Yes . . . ?"

"My . . . concentration, Your Majesty."

"Your concentration?"

Einhard looked extremely uncomfortable and seemed to be about to jump out of his chair. When he didn't speak, Charles tried again to prompt him.

"In what way, Einhard, did she disturb your concentration?"

Einhard hesitated again, and Charles could see droplets forming on his forehead. "I'm afraid I found her . . ." Einhard cleared his throat and squirmed in his chair. "I found her somewhat . . . charming."

"Indeed."

"I'm afraid I did, Your Majesty."

"I see." Charles put his hand on his chin and pretended to contemplate Einhard's words. "And this charm," he said at length, "this charm was distracting to you?"

Einhard worked his mouth, but no words were forthcoming.

"Would you say you felt yourself falling in love with her?" Charles asked.

Einhard jumped to his feet. "Oh, no, Your Majesty. I wouldn't say that. No, no, I wouldn't think of—"

"I have to agree with you," Charles said, deciding to interrupt him before he had an apoplexy. "She is somewhat charming, but she has begun her novitiate, you know. She plans to be a nun. Sit, sit," he said, pointing to the chair.

"I assumed as much," Einhard said.

"Her being a nun doesn't mean you can't be attracted to her, of course."

"But she is your nun, my lord."

That remark caught Charles by surprise. His hand returned to his chin and his brow involuntarily wrinkled. He could see the sour milk of worry clotting in Einhard's expression. "Do you think that's why I called her here?" he said at length. "To claim her as my own?"

"I gave no thought to why you called her here, Your Majesty, except that you said you wished to consult with her."

"Mmmm," Charles said. "I did say that, didn't I?"

"Yes, my lord. It was a wise decision, I believe. She has the wit and intelligence of a man."

"And she's charming as well."

Sweat thickened on Einhard's brow. "You must understand that I never had any intention of—"

"But you *did* find her charming."

"Yes, but—"

Charles's laughter cut him off. "I would have cause to worry if you hadn't found her charming and distracting. I would think you something less than a man. I found her so myself. And I believe that, in spite of her youth, she has a certain feminine wisdom I'll find useful."

"Of course," Einhard said, looking relieved.

"You have shown her to the guest quarters?"

"I have, Your Majesty."

"I wonder, did she appear as tired and road weary as you seem to be?"

"I . . . I'm afraid I can't say, my lord. I don't seem to have the knack of knowing . . . well, of knowing what a woman feels. Or thinks," he added. "But, given that they are the weaker sex, I would assume she is quite exhausted."

"Do you think that I should wait awhile before I summon her?"

"That would be my advice, Your Majesty."

"Very well, Einhard. Thank you. You've done me a great service. You may go now, and I suggest you rest before you work."

Einhard gave him a grateful look and murmured, "Yes, my lord. Thank you, my lord," as he bowed and left.

Charles chuckled after he had gone. He'd never seen Einhard so smitten before. But who could blame him? He, himself, had been equally attracted to the girl's charm and her sharp wit. A young, inexperienced man like Einhard would be rendered a complete idiot, Charles thought, remembering his own youth.

Amelia, he reminded himself once again, was even younger than Einhard. She would be much more inclined to think of him as a father, just as Einhard did, than as a lover. It mattered not, he thought, since he had no intention of taking a lover now, especially one who had chosen the path of a nun. Besides the fact that he had the caliph of Baghdad to watch, another war against the Saxons was brewing, and the bishop had sent a message of the coming meeting of the synod in Frankfurt. Along with all that, there was, as always, the day-to-day business of making laws and decisions for the kingdom.

Of course, he could admit he was attracted to her. He

could even admit that attraction played a part in bringing her here and that he enjoyed her company. He knew, as well, that he most certainly could take advantage of her intelligence. It was his prerogative as king to have anyone he wanted come to serve him, and it was her duty to come when he called.

He couldn't help wondering, though, if she would have refused to come had he not been king, or if she would prefer someone younger. Like Einhard. It could be she found his awkwardness and his inexperience attractive.

He would force such thoughts from his mind, and he would force himself not to think about her until later, after she had rested. Then, when the time was right, he would command her appearance. In the meantime, he would have a swim to help him relax.

He was about to leave the hall when the chamberlain appeared at the end of the big room.

He spoke. "Begging your pardon, Your Majesty."

"Yes?" Charles sounded annoyed. He was eager for his swim.

"Your visitor petitions an audience, Your Majesty."

"Tell all visitors I am indisposed. I will see no one until . . ." He saw her behind the chamberlain. She looked tiny and fragile, except that the way she held her head high and her back straight belied any fragility. She was still dressed in the plain robe, tied at the waist, that she'd worn when he saw her arrive with Einhard. It was the same attire she'd worn at the convent and when he'd first met her at the edge of the forest. For a brief moment he allowed himself to imagine what she would look like in a silk robe and adorned with the jewels from the Orient that his wives and concubines wore.

"I would see you now, Your Majesty," she said, stretching her lovely neck to see around the chamberlain. "If you will grant it. I have reason to hurry the audience."

"Ah, yes, Sister Amelia," he said, at the same time dismissing the chamberlain with a wave of his hand. He waited while she approached. She made her little curtsy and kept her eyes downcast—all very proper but somehow lacking in even the slightest hint of humility or acquiescence. He knew nothing of her background, but he could see that she had about her the air of the highborn.

"Your Majesty." Her voice was young. It reminded him of summer.

"What is it you wish from me, Sister Amelia?" He spoke without taking his eyes off her, which, at the moment, seemed impossible.

She lifted her head and looked at him. Her eyes, dark and flecked with a cold golden light, had the effect of freezing him in place, making any movement away from her unlikely.

"The question," she said in a voice that was now infused with granite and iron, "is, rather, what is it you wish of me?"

Her demeanor stunned him. She'd seized that moment and launched her demand with an expert aim.

"I am told you wish to consult with me regarding a family matter," she continued. "I will tell you first that I am not greatly experienced in matters of family, but if you believe my advice may be valuable, I will do my best. However, we must do this quickly. I have duties demanding my attention at the abbey, and I cannot tarry long here, since I face another two-day ride on my return."

Her seriousness amused him, but he dared not let her know it lest he offend her. "You are too busy to serve your king?" he asked. His question was more to test her wit than to discipline her.

Her response was quick. "I am a loyal subject and most happy to serve Your Majesty. I only request that you tell me how as quickly as possible, since it is also my duty to serve God."

He had to pretend to clear his throat to keep from smiling. "Very well," he said with as much seriousness as he could muster. "We can begin our discussions before supper. First, though, I will have a swim in the palace baths. I always find it relaxing, and it will help clear my mind for our discussion."

Her eyes widened. "Supper, my lord? We will have our discussion at supper? I . . . I was hoping to begin the journey back before dark."

"My dear Sister Amelia, you must learn to slow your pace. It's not fitting that any of us should hurry through life. Not when it is so short." Charles stood and stepped down from the platform as he spoke. Amelia moved aside quickly to allow him room, bowing her head at the same time. Charles stopped when he was even with her and reached a hand to lift her chin. "I said that we will *begin* our discussion tonight. Then you will sup with me, and perhaps we will continue the discussion at a later date." He dropped his hand and, still looking into her eyes, said, "I hope you will find your quarters here comfortable for the duration of your stay."

He saw defiance light up the gold in her eyes again. He knew she was boiling with protests she dared not speak. As he turned and walked away from her he couldn't stop a smile of anticipation of the pleasure her defiance and wit held for him.

6

Aix-la-Chapelle

Spring 794

Amelia

The king was being brutish, selfish, and unfair. He was, I supposed, acting like a king.

Certainly I was suspicious of his claim that he wanted to consult with me about any matter at all, since I was young, at least in comparison to his age, and I was inexperienced. I wondered why I had felt so attracted to him earlier.

I was, of course, mindful that my sisters in Christ at the abbey were suspicious his motives might be of a carnal nature. I considered that highly unlikely, since His Majesty already had a wife and, if the rumors were true, at least one concubine. Furthermore, if he had a sinful desire for another woman he could have his pick of practically any woman in the kingdom. There was no reason to think he would want a soon-to-be nun with a slight body, shorn hair, and a rather ordinary face.

I was quite certain his reason for bringing me to the palace was neither because of my wisdom nor my beauty but something else altogether. If only I could discover what it was, I could accomplish it and get back to the abbey in time to plant the crops and spend time in the library.

It angered me that he had all but ignored my initial plea to allow me to be done with my duties. He'd even hinted that I would be here for several days. Looking around at the apartment assigned to me, I suspected he may have thought he could bribe me with comfort. The room was the size of three of our cells at the abbey. The bed was thick with down and feathers and bore two coverlets—one of the finest white wool and one of blue silk, which to me seemed luxurious to the point of decadence. There was a large table in the room on which sat goblets of silver with a pitcher to match, along with a richly decorated pottery bowl. Besides the table and bed there were two chairs of carved wood and a chest, the contents of which I could not guess. All of it spoke of enormous wealth. I should not have been surprised. This was, after all, part of the palace of the king of the realm. Still, I had never even imagined such riches.

The room, to my surprise, was comfortably warm in spite of the cold bite of the spring wind blowing in from the east. There was no hearth in the room, not even a brazier. The chilling thought lodged in my mind that the room could have been warmed by the fires of hell. But then I remembered something I'd read recently about modern architecture: Special rooms could be built beneath a structure where fires burned to warm the rooms above.

It was wrong of me to think of the fires of hell anyway. They implied that the king was in league with the devil and could tap into his inferno for his own uses. Although I might find fault with him, I had to admit King Charles was known for his piety and his just laws and was not likely to be in league with the devil. Remembering that calmed my fears a little, but I still would not allow myself to enjoy the warmth. I wanted nothing to tempt me to stay, so I wrapped my cloak around my body and prepared to step out of my luxurious quarters into the courtyard.

Before I left the apartment, however, I couldn't resist raising the lid of the chest and peering inside. What I saw almost took the breath of life from me. A woman's robe of crimson silk trimmed with what must have been ermine and encrusted with gold ropes lay folded in the bottom. It was a garment fit for a queen—or for the king's concubine. I let go of the lid to the chest, letting it close with a thud, and stepped away from it quickly, as if it might somehow contaminate me. I had no idea why I would have been assigned a room holding such a garment; nor did I want to know. I pulled my wrap tighter and stepped out into the yard.

The spring wind with its leftover ice met me immediately. I stood, letting it surround me and baptize me with its sharpness, allowing it to wash away whatever meaning the crimson robe held.

When I opened my eyes and began a slow walk through

the courtyard, the first thing to catch my attention was a group of women approaching the royal quarters. The one in front was a bit rotund, as some women are inclined to be in their later years, and she was dressed in a blue robe of so fine a weave, it might have been spun water. The three women behind her appeared younger and wore robes of a gray color and coarse texture, though not so coarse as my own. The woman in blue sensed my gaze, and when she lifted her eyes and saw me, she paused for the briefest of moments, as if to study me, but gave me no greeting. Instead she quickly turned away, disappearing into the royal quarters with the three younger women.

It occurred to me that she must have been Queen Fastrada, whom the king married after the death of Queen Hildegard. He married each of them in order to form political alliances to strengthen his kingdom, and he was much admired by most of his subjects for his astuteness in choosing wives for that purpose. I knew little of the politics of such matters. I was, however, frequently exposed to the gossip of travelers who stopped at Münster-Bilzen for lodging, since Mother Landrada often assigned me as interpreter. They always seemed to know when the king had taken a new wife or a new concubine. He even had one of his wives, so I'd been told, banished to a convent because he wished to marry another. According to the gossips, the late Pope Stephen was much opposed to and angered by the king's actions, as well as his practice of keeping concubines. The fact that neither Stephen nor our current pope, Hadrian, dared confront

Charles was, according to these travelers, because they depended upon the king for the protection of Rome. If it is true that the sins of the mighty are more easily forgiven than the sins of the weak, may God the Father, Son, and Holy Spirit and all the saints protect us.

It occurred to me that it was not seemly for a woman intent on proclaiming herself a bride of Christ to contemplate such matters as the carnal sins of kings, nor to assume failure of judgment on the part of the Holy Father. It was best to spend my time in prayer, particularly since I had found it difficult to follow the vigilance of Saint Benedict and pray at the appointed times during my journey to the palace. Besides, as I mentioned, the king is known to be pious in all areas save those involving women.

Back in my assigned quarters, I did my best to pray as I knelt with my back to the chest. "Our Father, who art in Heaven, hallowed be . . ." Had the mother of God ever worn a silken robe the color of the horizon when the sun is low and . . . ? "Thy kingdom come, thy will be . . ." Our Lord Jesus Christ had worn a simple robe, not one of crimson silk. The queen's robe was a demure blue, so red must be the color worn by the women who warmed the king's bed in illicit . . . "Forgive us our trespasses. Forgive. Forgive. Forgive."

I tried to pray, oh, yes, how I tried. But I am a woman, born of a woman, and weak. I had never been tempted by crimson silk before. Never had cause to wonder how it would feel against my skin, whether it would compliment my dark hair and eyes.

At last a servant came to lead me back to the royal quarters. I followed him, feeling miserable, yet happy to be led away from temptation the color of the fires of hell.

As soon as I was shown into the room in the royal residence where the king sat, I knew I had merely been led from one level of hell to another.

Charles was seated in front of a fire of red tongues licking at the open chimney. He lounged in a large chair covered with the hide of an animal I supposed to be a bear. An identical chair waited opposite him. He sat up straighter and smiled when I entered.

"Amelia! Come, join me."

I walked toward him, and as I grew closer I could see that his hair, thick and luxurious, was still damp from his swim. A few droplets lingered, diamondlike, on his coarse burnt-ocher beard. I was in a trance, completely incapable of moving my eyes away from him. Had he not spoken to the servant—a few words of dismissal—I might have been sucked into his spell. It was not until the spell was broken that I noticed he was not dressed in the devil's crimson, as I'd half expected. Instead, he wore the same type of linen shirt and breeches he'd worn at the abbey, the simple dress of Frankish commoners.

I bowed, and he signaled for me to sit in the chair across from him. "I hope you found the afternoon restful," he said.

"I spent the afternoon in prayer," I said, immediately regretting how smug and pretentious I sounded.

He didn't respond. He simply looked at me with what I imagined to be the remnants of a smile on his lips. I was certain he could see through the thin veneer of my false piety.

"What is it you wish to discuss with me?" To my horror and regret, I realized too late that those words made me sound rude and disrespectful. I should have waited for him to reveal his wishes to me at his leisure. It was obvious now that I could very well be at risk of being thrown into a dungeon for disrespect.

Instead he laughed—little puffs of laughter. I was stunned. Was he making fun of me? Before I could decide whether or not to be angry, he spoke.

"You are the most impatient nun I've ever encountered. What pulls you with such force back to the abbey? Besides your prayers and meditation," he added, as if to ward off a burst of piety and self-importance on my part.

"It is time to prepare the soil," I said, then added, "my lord," as an afterthought, hoping to make amends for my brashness.

"Ah, yes, Lentzenmanoth," he said, using the Frankish name he had decreed the third month of the year to be called. "I find it hard to imagine you guiding the plow and the oxen," he said.

"Mother Landrada has given me the duty of overseeing the preparation of the fields, Your Majesty. The marling has just begun, and I hope to begin an experiment with manuring the soil. I believe it may help bring about greater yield. The soil, I believe, can become tired and worn and needs to be replenished, just as a human body or an animal does. Manure provides replenishment with the cast-off food of animals."

I had not meant to go on so long or in so much detail. It is only that my enthusiasm for the soil and its ability to produce in varying degrees of abundance made me overly talkative.

"Greater yield?" Charles said, leaning toward me with obvious interest. "Manuring and marling? I don't know of such things. How is it you know of them? Explain it to me."

I hesitated a moment, wanting to make sure he wasn't making fun of me, but his interest seemed genuine. I explained to him what I knew and how I learned most of it. Travelers from other lands gave me bits and pieces of information, and I did my best to put it together. Our discussion went on for several minutes, and because of my deep interest in the subject and the king's insightful questions, I almost forgot to be curious about the true reason he had sent for me. Furthermore, his genuine interest in the subject seemed to make him irresistibly attractive. It was not until another servant appeared in the room to announce that our meal awaited us that I realized how long we had been there talking in front of the fire.

"Ah, yes, supper awaits," the king said, reaching for my hand to help me up as he stood. "And we haven't even gotten to the primary matter I wished to discuss with you."

When he led me into the dining room, I was surprised to see such a large company already seated at the table.

Among those present was the woman in blue I had taken to be the queen. Charles went to her immediately and kissed her hand.

"Fastrada, my queen," he said. "I present to you Sister Amelia, whom I have summoned from Münster-Bilzen Abbey to advise me on matters of the court."

I bowed to her and murmured, "Your Highness," but she acknowledged me with only a tight mouth and a scrutinizing gaze. I was then presented to each of his six daughters, some of whom were very close to my own age and had children of their own. The two youngest girls, who must have been nine or ten years of age, were Fastrada's children. His three sons, who, the king said, ranged in age from fifteen to nineteen, were away governing the subkingdoms he had bequeathed them in Italy and Aquitaine. I knew he had a fourth son, his eldest, called Pepin the Hunchback, but he failed to mention him.

It was a noisy supper with much laughter and chattering and with the king's grandchildren climbing up onto his lap, kissing his face, pulling his beard, and screaming with delight when he bellowed with pretended pain. I found myself smiling at his antics as well. The older daughters laughed and gossiped among themselves, and the queen seemed quite absorbed with her two children, all of which left me generally unnoticed.

The meal was far more sumptuous than my abbey's usual fare. There was beef, roasted and pimentoed, and served on a large trencher of bread that had turned the color of redwood from the juices that dripped from the meat. There was also fish and a hen stuffed with spices, as well as a bowl of beans and leeks. I took a morsel of the meat-soaked bread and accepted a cup of what turned out to be exceptional wine. It was my intention to ignore the apples and pots of honey that had been placed near me on the table, but I failed miserably. I am overly fond of the taste of sweets and find so much pleasure in the way sweetness caresses my tongue, it must surely be a sin.

Once during the meal I saw the king glance at me and give me a nod and a smile and seem about to speak to me, but he was quickly distracted by one of the children. Otherwise I was left to myself and could have eaten two of the apples and even more of the honey without being noticed had I not been keenly aware of God peering down from heaven. I was preoccupied with inspecting the way my sticky fingers clung to one another when I became quite suddenly aware that everyone was looking at me. It took me a long, embarrassing moment to realize I was being bid a good night by the women and children.

"May God and his angels watch over each of you," I said, hiding my sticky fingers under the table.

When they all left, the queen turned back and spoke to Charles. "You will retire to our bed soon," she said. It was not a question but a command, which Charles ignored. He rose from his chair and turned his back to her, offering me his hand to help me up from the table. When he took my sticky hand he laughed.

"It seems I have become attached to you rather quickly," he said.

His remark caught me by surprise, and, without intending to do so, I laughed with him. He led me, with our hands attached by remnants of honey, back to the outer room, where the fire in the great hearth still danced and raged. To my relief as well as my embarrassment, he ordered a servant to bring a basin of water so that we were both able to remove the signs of my gluttony from our fingers.

His next statement, made as he tossed the drying cloth he had used to the floor, surprised me as much as his earlier remark.

"I'm afraid you found the meal distressing. It must have seemed like something akin to a brawl to you, since your meals at the abbey are customarily taken in silence."

"I had no expectations that dining in the palace would in any way resemble what I'm accustomed to at the abbey," I said. "And forgive me, Your Majesty, but you are mistaken. I was not distressed."

"Children don't annoy you?"

"Why do you ask?"

"Why did you not answer?"

"Your Majesty, it is quite obvious that you take great pleasure in your family. Including the children."

My response brought a smile to his face. "They are my greatest pleasure," he said, "but you still haven't answered my question."

"Sometimes children annoy me."

He laughed again—loud and hearty. "Your honesty both pleases and amuses me."

"If I may ask, Your Majesty, is that the matter you wished to discuss with me? Whether or not I find children annoying?"

My question sobered him, and he took a long time to reply. "The matter concerns one of my sons. The eldest, Pepin, known as the Hunchback."

"I know of him, of course. Everyone in the realm has heard of him, Your Majesty."

"And of his rebellion, I suppose." The king's expression became even graver.

I didn't respond, since I wasn't certain what I was allowed to acknowledge, although, of course, I'd heard of the Hunchback's rebellion. It was said he hatched the plot to overthrow his father and become king himself while Charles was at war with the Huns a few months earlier.

"I have spoken with Einhard about this," Charles said, "but he was of little help. Pepin must be punished for his betrayal, but I cannot kill or mutilate him. He was my firstborn." He was silent for a long moment, studying the fire, before he added in a hoarse whisper, "And I love him dearly." He glanced up at me. "I still think of him sometimes, remembering how, when he was no more than a baby, he would run to me with his arms out, laughing. I remember, too, how we worried when the sickness came that twisted his spine. I slept in his bed with him and held him while he cried and writhed with pain. I was not king enough to command the demon to leave."

The unshed tears I saw in his eyes surprised me, and surprised me a second time when they became sharp, glistening daggers that cut my heart. This man had loved his son. That made all the more puzzling the rumors that Pepin had rebelled because Charles had cruelly cut him out of the line of succession in favor of his younger brother.

The king looked away from me for a moment, collecting himself. "It has become clear to me that I need the advice of a woman," he said, turning back to me. The tears were gone, and only a bit of puff and redness lingered to rim his eyes. "I might under other circumstances speak with the queen, but she has long wanted Pepin out of the way, which, as you must see, renders her unable to help." I knew my face betrayed me when he added, "You are surprised? The gossipmongers have not gotten their teeth into that morsel?"

"I have heard nothing of the queen in regards to this, Your Majesty."

"And what have you heard?"

"That you pushed him out of the line of succession in favor of his brother."

The king managed a small, sad smile. "I knew I could trust you to be ruthlessly truthful."

"I mean no offense, Your Majesty."

"None was taken. I did push him out," he said, surprising me again.

"Then you must understand his rebellion."

"I do, indeed." The sadness crept back into his voice. "Fastrada was cruel to him. Jealous, perhaps, because she had no sons of her own. She taunted him with her declarations that he would never be king because he was frail and misshapen. I was weak in that I didn't stop her."

"You were afraid of her?" I saw a look of surprise or alarm in his eyes, and I immediately wished I could take back my words. I should never have suggested the king was afraid. Obviously he'd made a poor choice in summoning me, since I could do nothing more than make mistake after mistake.

"I didn't stop her because I was considering passing him over. But not for the reasons she suggested. I wanted to protect him."

"You thought him weak?"

"No. I wanted to protect him because he is a bastard."

I found myself unable to speak. After a pause, during which the king appeared to be fighting back tears again, he continued.

"His mother was my concubine before I ever took a wife. I had to put her aside when I married at my mother's behest in order to form an alliance with the Lombards. Pepin's mother resides now in the monastery at Nevelles."

I saw, by the slump of his shoulders and the way his eyes fixed on something he could not see, that he had loved this woman in a way that he could never love the wives he married for reasons of political alliances. I saw, too, that he had wanted to protect his son from the furor that would arise if a bastard whose mother did not come from a powerful family ascended to the throne.

"In trying to protect him, I have brought him harm," the king said. "I cannot harm him more by killing him or mutilating him or tossing him into a dungeon prison to rot."

I watched agony and love rack his spirit, and I understood for the first time that only the formidably strong can survive the monarchy. I ached for him and for his son, and I admired him more than ever. Finally I was able to speak.

"You must have him shorn and sent to a monastery."

The king, whose chin had sunk to his chest, raised his eyes to look at me.

"He will be shorn so that his shame will speak to the kingdom," I said. "By that action the people will know that usurping the throne is not tolerated. His hair will grow again, as is God's plan, for our Father in heaven knows we are not meant to live in shame forever. You will send him to a monastery because he will be safe, and because it is a place where his mind and soul will continue to grow. In time he will see that it is out of love for him that you placed him there, and perhaps eventually he will know that being loved makes a man richer than having a kingdom to rule. However, when you speak to him again, you do so in a manner that leads him to choose the monastery as if it were his own idea."

There was a long silence, and I felt I had overstepped my rights yet again. I should have phrased everything differently. I should not have made my thoughts sound so much like a command, but more like a suggestion.

"My little nun," the king said finally, startling me. "You have spoken with the wisdom of an elder."

He smiled at me, and I relaxed somewhat, and rejoiced as well, since, now that I had done my duty for the king, I could get back to the abbey, the farm, and the library. I was even basking in the pride of my own wisdom that the king had lauded. In the next moment, however, I was reminded that I was nothing more than one of the king's subjects and perhaps not nearly as wise as I thought.

"The hour is late, and you must be tired after your journey," the king said. "If you don't find your quarters satisfactory, you must tell me. I want you well rested and comfortable during your long stay."

7

Aix-la-Chapelle

Spring 794

Amelia

I was shocked the next morning when I realized it was almost dawn when I awoke. I didn't remember ever sleeping so late, and I'm not certain what made me do it this time. Perhaps it was that I slept very little during the journey to the palace, or perhaps it was the soft bed of down and feathers that made me feel as if I were on a heavenly cloud.

As soon as I dressed, I hurried to the chapel I had seen earlier on the palace grounds. I would recite the scriptures and prayers that should have been said three hours earlier while the sky was still dark. The chapel, with its high dome, was the most beautiful I'd ever seen. It was built of stone in an octagon shape. There were sixteen tiers of arches surmounted by a gallery. There were marble colonnades that I knew must have been imported from Rome. There were mosaics of Christ and the twenty-four old men of the Apocalypse. I found it difficult to close my eyes to pray because of the temptation in the beauty that surrounded me.

Before I finished the ritual of vigiliae, I sensed another presence in the church behind me. Someone had entered to pray, I thought, but I willed myself not to turn around until I had finished. When at last I stood and turned toward the door, I saw Einhard standing just inside the chapel. He must have been praying, because he made the sign of the cross and took a few steps toward me and bowed. At first I thought he was paying reverence to the Host, until I realized he had bowed to me.

"Amelia," he murmured. His voice trembled and he seemed to choke on the sound of my name.

"Yes?" I walked toward him.

"The king has asked me to deliver a message to you."

A moment of hope lightened my steps. No doubt the king accepted that I had accomplished my duty and could now be on my way home.

"His Majesty asked me to tell you that you are welcome to break your fast in the palace dining room with his family, and—"

"How kind of him," I said. "But please tell him I require only the simplest of meals, which I can prepare myself if need be. Tell him also that I prefer to dine alone so that I can have more time to pray and meditate." I didn't add that I also wanted to avoid the discomfort I felt at being the outsider at family gatherings.

By this time I had walked the entire length of the chapel, and the closer I got to the odd little man, the more agitated he became.

"I am not able . . . no, I am quite able, of course, but I won't . . . well, it's not that I won't. The truth is I cannot. . . . Not because I don't wish to do your bidding, of course, but . . ."

"Perhaps it would help if you paused a moment and took a deep breath." I placed my hand on his fidgeting and fluttering hand as I spoke. My touch seemed to alarm him. He jerked his hand away as his eyes widened, and he appeared to have trouble breathing.

"Yes. Yes, of course," he said. He took several quick, shallow breaths. "I . . . I only meant to say that I can't give the king your . . . The king is gone. He's not here. Not at the palace, I mean."

"He's gone? Where? For how long?" Despair seeped into my veins. If the king was away on some mission for his kingdom, I could be trapped in the palace for days. It could even be months, since the tentacles of his realm stretched from Rome to Hamburg and from the border of Moravia to the ocean where Gaul ends and dragons dwell.

"There is to be a council of bishops in Frankfurt," Einhard said, "to deal with certain heresies—"

"Frankfurt? He's gone to Frankfurt? That could take weeks!" My despair turned to anger.

Einhard's eyes were wide and his mouth bloodless with what I took to be alarm at my display. "I didn't mean to imply that His Majesty has gone to Frankfurt. I only meant to say that there is to be a council of bishops there in a few months to consider certain matters of faith. He has gone to consult with the bishop at Cologne in preparation for the meeting."

"I see." I spoke with as much calm as I could muster, trying to restore some of my dignity.

"He should be gone no more than a few days. A week at the most." Einhard backed away from me as he spoke. It both saddened and confused me that he was so uncomfortable in my presence.

"Thank you," I said, hoping he would take the hint and dismiss himself.

He looked at me for a moment with an expression I couldn't decipher except that he seemed to be miserable. Finally he turned away and left without another word. After that, it was I who stood motionless, not knowing what to do. Was I to be at Aix-la-Chapelle forever? How would the crops fare at Münster-Bilzen while I was gone? How was I to keep up with my mission of self-education? What about Mother Landrada? Her health was poor; would she survive until I returned?

Those thoughts and many more were vaulting and hurdling through my mind as I walked out of the chapel and into the courtyard. I knew immediately I should have stayed inside to pray and meditate to calm the turmoil in my soul. I ignored that small bit of wisdom, however, and gave in to irritability and frustration, as well as, I must admit, hunger.

I marched with emotionally fueled energy across the entire courtyard to the entrance to the royal apartments. By now I was so angry it mattered little to me whether or not I was accepted by the family or whether anyone spoke to me. I would not be uncomfortable in their presence. Let them be uncomfortable in mine. Great were my sins of anger and arrogance.

I was immediately admitted into the entrance hall with no questions asked, and I walked with briskness and purpose to the dining room. I was invited to dine with the royal family, and I expected everyone would be there when I arrived. I was surprised to see only one of the king's daughters present. I remembered her name was Bertha. She was seated at the table with a suckling infant and another child, a little girl, who I thought was around three years of age.

"Mama, look!" the child said. "She's here again."

Bertha raised her eyes from her baby to look at me. "Yes, I see. It's our father's nun."

Her eyes followed me as I seated myself at the table, which made me uncomfortable in spite of my earlier vow not to be. As soon as I was seated, a cup of goat's milk and a loaf of bread were placed in front of me by a servant. I looked around for the honey, but there was none this time.

"The others won't be here for some time. When the king is away, they all sleep late." Bertha laughed and shifted the baby from her left breast to her right. "I would be sleeping as well were it not for this little one. He wakes me too early every morning."

In spite of that complaint, she looked at the infant's face with great fondness and even picked up one of his soft, pliable hands to kiss his fingers. She seemed kind and gentle enough that I began to lose some of my animosity toward the family.

"You are not yet a nun, are you?" she said. "I can tell by the color of your habit that you are only a novice."

I waited until I completed my prayer for blessing of the food and made the sign of the cross before I answered her.

"I have not yet taken my vows."

"It is said the king brought you here for your wisdom?" She put so much emphasis on that last word that I wondered if she was implying I must have, in reality, been summoned for another reason.

"His desire was to consult with me on certain matters." I almost said, *matters regarding his family*, but thought better of it. I didn't wish her to be suspicious that I would be privy to any family secrets.

"You are so wise at such a young age that the king consults with you? Your education must be superior. Usually he consults with Einhard or Alcuin, the old master teacher. What is your abbey? Perhaps I should send my son there for his own education."

"I was given to Münster-Bilzen Abbey at a very young age." Although I knew it was wrong, I spoke with a great deal of pride. It flattered me that she assumed I was so wise.

"Ah! Münster-Bilzen, you say?"

There was such fervor in her remark that surprise and

curiosity overcame my pridefulness. All I could manage was a weak, "Yes. You've heard of it?"

"Heard of it? Indeed I have," she said with a merry little chuckle. "The king has promised it to me. I am to be the next abbess. I understand the current one is quite elderly."

My appetite fled. So stunned was I that I was only dimly aware of the words she spoke after that. She said something about having heard the current abbess was very religious, although she was only a lay abbess, and that, except for the past two years of drought, the abbey had been quite profitable.

We must have had some form of conversation that followed, but I remember none of it. I remember only my desire to leave the dining room as soon as possible. I had no idea where I would go, but Bertha's remarks left me feeling as if the walls were closing in and suffocating me.

When at last I was outside the residence, I lingered for a while in the courtyard. I hoped the spring wind that swirled around me and spat a few weak drops would numb me enough that I would not feel the raging and frothing of the demons Disappointment and Anger who possessed me. I knew I should have gone back to the chapel and begged for forgiveness for allowing the demons to invade my soul, but the truth was, may God forgive me, I was not willing to let them go.

The king must have taken me for a fool. I made no secret of the fact that I hoped to be abbess of Münster-Bilzen one day, and that all my work, study, and actions were done in preparation for that. He knew my ambition, while at the same time knowing the abbey was promised to his daughter. What kind of wicked cruelty did he possess that he would not tell me that my dream was impossible? Which side of him was his true side? The one that made him weep because a son he loved betrayed him, and who showed such fond indulgence for his grandchildren? Or the one that made him enjoy the pitiless act of deceiving me?

My purpose to him was nothing more than to provide him a few moments of amusement.

Because of my emotions, I walked around the palace grounds for a long time doing nothing more than allowing the cold wind to strike my face. I must have made a dozen rounds at least before I realized that the palace and the settlement around it had awakened and begun to stir. As was true of Münster-Bilzen, a town had grown up just outside the walls that surrounded the palace grounds. I could hear the shouts of peasants to their livestock, the sound of merchants crying out the virtues of their wares, and I could imagine clerks running about with their wooden styluses and their ink-stained fingers.

Before long, I saw some of the people pass through the gate to the palace grounds—those very clerks I had imagined, along with what I took to be tradesmen and artisans who would do their duties to keep the palace running. While I watched, I saw Einhard enter the gate, wrapped in a long cloak to protect him against the cruel wind. I realized then that his residence must have been one of the large walled edifices I had seen as he guided me to the palace grounds when we first arrived. Once inside the walls of the palace compound, he entered one of the long wooden buildings opposite the royal apartments.

I had no idea what those buildings housed. Although my curiosity was aroused, I was reluctant to follow him inside to investigate, since my very presence seemed to agitate and distress him. It was only a moment later that I saw some of the children, whom I now knew to be the king's children and grandchildren, walk out of the residence and into the same long building Einhard had entered. A gust of curiosity blew around me, mingling with the wind and entering my mind like the swirling malicious spirits Mother Landrada told me inhabited her Saxon homeland. I was compelled to follow the children inside.

They passed through an entrance hall and into a room furnished with long benches. I remained in the entrance hall, but I could see Einhard at one end of the adjoining room standing on a raised podium. A frown of concentration puckered his brow as he studied a book on the table in front of him. He seemed not to notice that the children chattered and twittered as they sat themselves on the benches—a short row of boys in front and two rows of girls in the back.

As soon as Einhard raised his eyes from the book, the children grew quiet and picked up wax tablets and wooden styluses that had been placed on the floor before they entered. He smiled at them, apparently pleased by their manners. I had never seen him smile before, nor seen his shoulders relaxed nor his hands as still as they were now.

He spoke to the group in Latin, bidding them good morning, and they replied to him in Latin with the same greeting. He then passed the book he had been studying to one of the boys and asked him to read. The boy, standing in front with Einhard, read the text, which I recognized as a fable by Phaedrus. The child read the Latin with a Frankish accent, but when he was questioned by Einhard to tell him in his own language what he had read, his interpretation was flawless.

I was so captivated that I stayed to watch, out of sight, while Einhard had each student, including the girls, read and translate from Latin. Later, I was amazed when he began an oral lesson in arithmetic.

"My child," he said to the girl who appeared to be the oldest of all the students, "a mother says to her son, 'If you live as long again as you have already lived and yet as long again, then half as much plus a year, you will be a hundred years old.' Now, I ask you, my child, how old was her son?"

The girl picked up her waxen tablet and made a series of marks before she responded. "The son is a young man of sixteen and one-half years, Master Einhard."

Einhard was pleased and rewarded her with a compliment to her wisdom. I was equally pleased to see that a child of my own sex was given such an education even without being sent to a monastery.

I continued to watch for several minutes until I noticed

that the children were growing restless. Einhard apparently noticed the same, and, to my surprise, he suggested they all leave the schoolroom to run about the palace grounds, then bade them return when they saw him in the doorway. Never in the course of my childhood education at the abbey had I or any of my fellow students been dismissed to run or play or find other amusements for a short time when we grew restless. I was contemplating how wise this was on Einhard's part when it occurred to me that I should leave immediately, lest he find me in the entry hall and know that I had been observing the school.

It was too late. Einhard followed the children out of the classroom and saw me before I could leave.

"Good morning, sir," I said and tried to think of some plausible explanation for being there. All I could manage was an embarrassing stammer. I needn't have worried, since Einhard was obviously even more ill at ease than I. He kept opening and closing his mouth as if he wished to speak but could not. Finally I gathered my wits enough to attempt to ease the uncomfortable moment.

"I was very much impressed with your teaching," I said.

He still was not able to respond, so I tried again.

"I was also greatly surprised as well as pleased to see that you have included girls in the class. That was a wise and generous decision on your part."

"That was His Majesty's wish." Einhard's voice sounded choked and squeaky, but at least he managed to speak. "The king says it is equally important for females to be educated as for males, and he even gives them access to his library. At first I thought it strange that the king would expect females to be educated, but now I see the wisdom in it. Females, though weak-minded, can be trained."

"Indeed!"

Einhard's face turned red and he lowered his gaze and turned aside, hurrying back to his classroom. Deciding it would be cruel for me to prolong his agony by trying to continue the conversation, I left the building. I wanted to ask him where the king's library was located. Watching him teach the children made me hunger even more to get back to my studies. If I could find the library, perhaps I could find some books that would be of some benefit.

The library, as it happened, was easy to find. It was located next to the school. I knew its reputation, but it was far and above what I expected. I felt as if I had stumbled upon a great treasure. There were books on rhetoric, dialectics, astronomy, mathematics, architecture, philosophy, and Christianity, as well as tomes of poetry. The library was, of course, far superior to the one at the abbey, and seeing it strengthened the enigma that was King Charles. He was a great lawgiver and obviously an enthusiast of learning, and he wanted others to be educated, including females. He appeared to be capable of great affection for his family. I had seen him weep for love of his son. He was known to be a pious man who had instituted a death penalty for Saxons who did not keep the Sabbath. Yet at the same time he was ruthless in war and could be insensitive to the feelings and needs of others, including my own. Worst of all, he had deceived me by giving me false hope of being the abbess of Münster-Bilzen, when all along he knew it would go to his daughter.

I opened the book of the *Confessions of Saint Augustine* and began to read, trying once again to quell the sin of anger.

8

AIX-LA-CHAPELLE

SPRING 794

Amelia

The king returned within three days. I saw him ride through the gates on his magnificent horse in the early morning before the sun climbed above the horizon and just as I exited the chapel after my morning prayers.

I stopped, unable to take my eyes from him. His head and shoulders rose above all the men in his entourage. He wore a vest of otter skin to protect him against the cool spring weather and a cloak of royal blue that made him appear even broader of shoulder than usual. He dismounted with an easy grace and made his way toward the royal apartments while one of his men saw to his horse. I heard the clanking of his sword as he walked and saw him place his hand on its silver hilt. He must have sensed me looking at him, because he turned toward the chapel. I turned away quickly and hurried to my assigned quarters.

He was attractive, I could not deny that, but it was unseemly for me, a betrothed bride of Christ, to be so affected by his presence. For that reason, I resolved that I would not join the family for breakfast, as had been my custom for the last three days.

I had come to enjoy the company of the king's family in his absence, as his daughters and grandchildren became more accustomed to my presence and drew me into their conversations. The daughters, I found, were well educated and capable of conversing on a number of topics ranging from poetry and religion to the politics of the realm. I made it a point not to allow Bertha to guess that I had long wanted to be the abbess of the monastery that would be given to her. My anger was never directed at her, but I still found it difficult to forgive the king for not telling me the abbey had already been promised.

Later in the day, one of the court pages approached me as I was about to enter the library. I expected him to greet me with a summons to appear before the king, but I was surprised and perhaps even a little disappointed to learn it was not the king who wished to see me but one of his stewards. I was to meet him in the palace.

When I arrived, a man dressed in the clothes of a common laborer stood before the great fireplace where the king and I had sat earlier. As I walked toward him, the man bowed and spoke two words.

"My lady."

"Are you the one the king has asked to speak with me?" I asked as I approached him.

"I am to take you to the garden, my lady. Or should I address you as Sister?" he asked, eyeing my plain robe.

"I'm only a novice. I have not yet taken the veil," I said.

"Then I shall address you as my lady. I am to take you first to the garden and then to the orchard and following that the royal wheatfields."

"The king has ordered this?" I asked, surprised.

"He has indeed," the workman said. He took my arm and led me out the door. "The king says you will be able to advise us on new methods for growing crops, and he says I am to explain to you our method of crop rotations."

As I walked through the royal gardens and talked with the steward, I forgot my resentment for being pulled away from my work at the abbey. I was captivated by the rose garden and the buds that were already on the bushes. I had never been successful with roses at the abbey and was interested in the steward's explanation of pruning and grafting.

The vegetable garden paled in comparison to mine, however, and it was my turn to instruct him on the new art of manuring. We even went to the stables for dried manure and worked some of it into the soil the way the traveler from Gaul taught me.

I learned even more about grafting plants when we went to the apple orchard. However, as it happened, I knew more about rotating crops than the steward, and he seemed pleased to have me teach him.

So interested was I in all that we discussed, I was unwilling to return to the palace to eat and took my noon meal with the steward in the fields outside the gates. Later, when I saw the red ball of the sun sinking into the earth, I realized it was time for vespers. I had forgotten my obligations for the liturgical hours all day long. I was about to take my leave from the steward, whose name I'd learned was Rodolph, when I saw the king's servant approaching.

The servant bowed and spoke. "His Majesty, the king, requires your presence, Sister Amelia."

Earlier in the day I might have been offended that the king waited so long to send for me. Now, however, I was only slightly annoyed, not because he had waited so long but because I wanted time to wash myself and pray before going to bed.

"Please tell His Majesty that I am indisposed and request that he see me early tomorrow," I said.

"That is impossible, Sister. The king will see you now." The emphasis he put on that last word left me no other choice.

"Then tell him I will come to the palace after I have had time to wash my—"

"The king will see you now!" There was even more emphasis on the last word.

I paused a moment to quiet my spirit before I spoke. "Very well. I will see the king."

As I walked with the servant toward the palace gates, I made an attempt to shake some of the dust from my robe and rubbed my hands over my face, hoping to wipe away the grime collected there. I feared the scent of the manure I'd worked into the soil still lingered around me, but I could do nothing more than tell myself that if the king was offended by the scent, it was no one's fault but his own, since he'd given me no time to wash.

We entered the palace, and I saw the king was once again seated in front of the frolicking fire. As before, his hair and beard were still wet from cavorting in the royal baths. He smiled when he saw me, a smile that embraced me and pulled me toward him. As I drew closer I could see that weariness marred his face, especially around his eyes.

"Your Majesty," I said as I bowed before him.

"Ah, Amelia!" He extended one of his large, battle-hardened hands toward me and picked up my hand, brought it to his lips, and brushed it with a kiss. That touch turned my blood to intoxicating wine, but I forced myself to speak and break the spell.

"You wished to see me, my lord?"

"Yes, yes. Please sit down." He motioned toward the chair opposite him, where I had sat before. He noticed that I was hesitant. "Is something wrong?"

"I have been in the fields all day, Your Majesty. I have not had time to wash, and I don't wish to offend you with my—"

He laughed, interrupting me. "My nose is numbed every

day by men who smell of sweat and horses and their own piss and excrement. A woman like you, who is hardly more than a girl, could not possibly offend me. Sit! Sit!"

I did his bidding, sinking into the confines of the bearskin-covered chair. It was not until then that I realized the day in the fields had left me tired. I accepted with gratitude the cup of wine offered me by a servant who appeared out of nowhere.

"Tell me," the king said, "were you able to show Rodolph some of the farming techniques you told me about?"

"We shared our knowledge. I believe we learned from each other." It annoyed me that he was acting as if he had never misled me about the abbey, and I am certain it showed in my voice.

Nevertheless, the king kept plying me with questions. Of course I was compelled to respond, but I kept my answers as short as possible and said only that we had discussed crop rotations and fertilizer. My greatest desire at that moment was to tell him I was tired and wished to retire for the evening. That is hardly the kind of thing one says to the king, however. I had to find a more careful way of getting what I wanted.

"You've been away in Cologne, Your Majesty. You must be tired. I'm sure you'll want to go to bed soon."

"Tired?" he said. "Not at all. I always feel refreshed as well as relaxed after I've had a swim in the baths. You should try it yourself."

I knew not what to say. It came as a shock to me that he

would suggest the baths for me. That was a man's sport. I had never heard of women swimming in the baths as noblemen did, or in the rivers and lakes as peasant men did.

"My daughters and the children amuse themselves in the shallowest pools from time to time," he said, as if he'd read my mind. "The water is quite warm. You would enjoy it."

Once again I didn't know how to respond. It would be unseemly for me to play naked in the water, even with only women and children. I was quite sure Mother Landrada would not be pleased.

The king, I noticed, was looking at me with an odd expression, as if something was troubling him. I dared not speak again. My last attempt at turning the conversation resulted in the opposite of what I'd wanted.

The king cleared his throat and shifted in his chair. I was beginning to think I was making him as uncomfortable as I made Einhard. The thought pleased me, since, as I have confessed, I was still feeling resentful.

"My visit with the bishop of Cologne was fruitful," he said.

I nodded.

"I would have had him come to me, as is customary, but he is an old man now, and travel is difficult for him."

"I see."

The king paused again for another long moment. I believe it was as clear to him as to me that our encounter had become awkward.

"But the meeting was fruitful, as I mentioned," he said. There was another long pause before he added, "I wanted his insight on the Arian question."

"The Arian question? Is that what the Frankfurt meeting is to be about?" His last remark had piqued my interest, and I couldn't help inquiring in spite of my resentment.

"That and more. You've heard of it? This Arian heresy?"

"Of course I have," I said. "The question is an old one, three hundred years old, at least. If I am to be an abbess, it should quite naturally concern me." I made the last remark as bait for him.

"Ah, yes, of course," he said, not taking the bait. "You know, of course, that the doctrine questions the Trinity."

"Yes, I know. The Arians hold that Jesus could not be equal with God, since God is the Father, and he existed before Jesus the Son. But that was decided at the Nicene Council. What is the bishop's opinion?"

"He agrees with me, of course. He says they are wrong, that Father, Son, and Holy Spirit are one." The king gave me a questioning look. "I'm sure you agree."

When the king saw that I was slow in responding, he said, "You do agree, don't you?"

"Am I to answer truthfully, or am I to risk being called an apostate?"

"You don't agree that the Father and Son and Holy Spirit are one?" He seemed genuinely alarmed.

My mouth was dry from the fear that arose in me. "One should always agree with the king," I said.

His hand came down hard on the arm of his chair, and I saw his eyes flash. "Why will you not give me a direct and truthful answer?"

His sudden show of anger somehow emboldened me. "The truth, Your Majesty, is that the Arian argument does seem to follow logic. However, perhaps the nature of religion is to rely on faith, not logic." I could see immediately that my answer did not sit well with him.

"You speak in circles. How am I to make sense of that?"

It seemed prudent not to answer that question. The king kept looking at me for a moment with that fire in his eyes until the fire seemed no more than dancing lights, and laughter rumbled in his throat.

"You are a most unusual woman," he said.

That was an unexpected remark. "I don't see how," I said.

"Because of the way you use your mind," he said. "You reason well. You seem to want to investigate everything, and you are wise."

"That is no more uncommon in a female than in a male, my lord. If you see it less, then perhaps women merely live up to what men expect of them and are not allowed to be educated."

He laughed again. "Perhaps you are right. I agree with you that women should be educated. My own daughters were given that benefit. They've been given every benefit."

"Except the right to marry," I said.

"I love them so much I couldn't bear to have them leave the court, and if they married they would surely—"

I couldn't stop a laugh from erupting. The king gave me a puzzled, questioning look.

"Forgive me," I said. "I should not have—"

"What do you mean by that derisive laugh?" His expression was still more one of curiosity than anger.

"Nothing. I—"

"Tell me!"

"I . . . umm . . . I'm afraid I don't believe that is really your motive for not allowing your daughters to marry, Your Majesty."

"Then what is my motive?"

"Could it be that you are afraid a son-in-law would try to take your throne from you?"

He was silent for a long time, and I began to fear he was attempting to come up with a suitable punishment for my irreverence. Finally he spoke. "With a mind like yours, you should have a kingdom of your own to rule."

"That is a privilege that was not given to me," I said. "The most I can hope for is to oversee the small kingdom of an abbey." I watched his face carefully to see if he would take the bait this time. He did not.

"I can see that you are ambitious," he said. Then with a laugh, he added, "We see both the light and the dark of each other's souls because our souls have mingled."

I was a bit startled by the thought of our souls mingling, but before I could reply he spoke again. "That ambition is not so unusual. Every noblewoman wishes for the same thing," he said.

"But not for the same reason." I leaned forward in my chair to make certain he understood. "I don't wish to be named an abbess only for the rents I will garner. I wish to make the abbey thrive for the glory of God, and because it is the only opportunity I see to challenge my mind. I don't wish to appoint an overseer but to be involved myself."

"You want to be a ruler, albeit of a small kingdom." There was a hint of condescension in his voice.

"I want to be able to put my talents and my education to good use and not to sit idle," I said with a measure of resentment. "I'm certain you understand, since you would not want your own talents to go unused."

"It never occurred to me to sit idle, nor to allow any talent I might have to go to waste," he said.

"What you take for granted, a woman must fight for."

"Mmmm," he said with a thoughtful frown. I believed for a moment he understood my position, but in the next moment, I doubted. "There is fire in your belly," he said, and I could not tell whether he meant to be complimentary or mocking.

Whatever his motivation, the remark brought a darkness to my soul. I sat silent and thinking that no matter how hot the fire in my belly burned, I was losing the fight to reach my goal.

"Come sup with me," the king said, rising from his chair. "I'm afraid I've waited so late that the family has left the dining room, and I detest eating alone." He reached for my hand to help me from the chair. "Come," he said, "and I'll fill your ears with the dull stuff to be discussed at the council meeting in Frankfurt, and you will see that being a ruler and making decisions is not always so interesting as you might think."

He was wrong. It all sounded fascinating to me. I had to keep prodding him for more. He told me of his plan to set a maximum price for food in order to give the people of the realm relief from the famine of the previous year. He spoke of a proposal from the bishops, which he supported, that would require education of the clergy in Latin. He said he would also seek to prohibit the adoration of images. He claimed it was akin to the pagan idolatry that was still rampant in the kingdom. In spite of the brevity of his explanations, I could see how the council of bishops and the king formed a governing body. The king followed by issuing laws to enforce their decisions.

"I'm boring you," the king said, filling his wine cup again for the fourth or fifth time. He had eaten little. "We'll talk of something else." His weariness was replaced by a mellow lethargy as he leaned back in his chair with his cup of wine.

"I'm not bored, Your Majesty. I am envious," I said.

His laughter was a much softer, quieter sound this time. "Don't you know, my little nun, that envy is a sin?"

"*Omnes enim peccaverunt et egent gloriam Dei,*" I said.

He smiled. "We have all sinned and come short of the glory of God." He studied my face for several seconds. "I almost wish I was not compelled to fight the Saxons again so I could come back here after the council and spend hours conversing with you."

"Must you fight the Saxons?" I wanted to add that I would enjoy more hours conversing with him, but I dared not.

"I must. It is my duty as king to subdue them for the kingdom and to bring them salvation." His face was sad as he spoke.

"I'm sure you know many of them aren't true Christians and go back to their old gods," I said. "That's because your method of bringing them to salvation is . . ."

"Is what?" he asked when he saw I had censored myself.

I shook my head. I had no right to say what I was thinking.

"Tell me. I command you."

He'd said the last with a smile, so that I wasn't certain he was serious. But I dared not risk that he wasn't. "Your method is to slaughter them if they don't accept baptism and Christianity," I said.

"Yes?"

By now I was wondering why I seemed perpetually to say things I shouldn't. Why couldn't I be wise enough to stop now? "Accepting Christianity on threat of death hardly seems a true conversion," I blurted. "A person will declare anything to avoid death."

He frowned and was quiet again, thinking about it. "There is hardly time for sermons and catechism on a battlefield," he said. "And you surely know the Lord commanded us to baptize pagans."

"Dico tibi nisi quis renatus fuerit ex aqua et Spiritu non potest introire in regnum Dei," I said, quoting from the Gospel of John about the need to be baptized in the Spirit as well as water, hoping it would be a compromise.

He smiled a little wearily. "I can only hope they are baptized in the Spirit," he said. Then, standing, he once again pulled me to my feet. "Come with me outdoors. I feel too confined. I would see the stars."

I let him lead me to the courtyard, grateful to be out of the confines of the palace. He seemed to grow more and more relaxed and kept up a stream of conversation as we walked.

"You speak Latin like a bishop," he said. "I don't expect simple clerics to speak as well as you, but the language is not so difficult that they can't learn it. I'm not asking them to memorize grammar, you see. I only want to prevent the kind of barbarisms a priest in the village outside the palace walls made. He baptized my newest grandson *in nominee patria et filia.* In the name of the nation and the daughter."

This time I couldn't keep from laughing with him. Perhaps it was the wine I had consumed or the embrace of the crisp night air, or the fact that I was tired from my day in the fields, but I felt relaxed and maybe even a little giddy. In spite of my considerable effort to remain angry and resentful, I was enjoying myself, and so was Charles. We were laughing as we walked farther out into the courtyard, until at one point I stumbled on a wooden horseshoe one of the mounts in the king's retinue had lost.

Charles was quick to catch me before I hit the ground, and the awkward movement on the part of both of us only made us laugh harder. He didn't let go as he helped me right myself. Instead he held me and pulled me close to him. I could feel his breath on my face and lips, and a strange sensation of some unseen force pulling us together. I knew that he felt it as well. I thought for a moment that he would kiss me, and what is worse, I wanted him to. But I pulled away. I couldn't turn from him, though, not at first. I could only back away, unable to take my eyes from him.

"Amelia," he said, reaching a hand toward me as if to bring me back.

"Good night, Your Majesty," I said and finally turned away, moving with as much resolve as I could manage toward my apartment. I felt puzzled that I could have, even for a brief moment, the kind of feelings I'd just experienced. It was even more puzzling that those feelings would be directed toward a man who had taken away my hopes and dreams.

9

Aix-la-Chapelle

Spring 794

Charles

Charles knew he should be tired enough to sleep after the long journey, the relaxing swim, and more wine than he usually drank. But sleep was elusive.

It was the young woman—the little nun—that filled his thoughts and kept him awake. He knew she was upset about something, but he had no idea what. Perhaps, he thought, it was because he'd left for Cologne without telling her good-bye. He decided that wasn't likely, since she hadn't wanted to come to the palace at all. It was obvious she didn't care whether he was here or halfway across the world in the Avars.

Was it that he had interrupted her day in the fields with Rodolph? It couldn't be that. It was late and time for her to come back from the fields anyway. Was it that she didn't like her lodgings? If that was the case, why didn't she just say so? Besides, she was preparing to be a nun, so she was used to the barest of furnishings and the most uncomfortable of beds.

Her mood had warmed some for a while during the evening. She was even laughing and enjoying herself at one point, and he was almost certain she'd wanted him to kiss her. But not completely certain. He'd been unsure enough that he did not follow through.

Perhaps she hadn't wanted him to kiss her at all. Perhaps he'd misread her, since she did seem to return to her dark mood rather quickly. Or was that because he *hadn't* kissed her?

Now he had a headache. Because of too much wine, he thought. Or too much uncertainty about Amelia's moods. He had to stop worrying about it and making it seem so difficult. After all, women were simple creatures, easy to please with a few baubles and fine silks.

That thought almost made him laugh. Sometimes baubles and silks didn't please them. Sometimes they didn't seem so simple. Especially not Amelia. She was not only intelligent and educated; she was also a woman. Those three factors combined in one person made her impenetrable. In the intellectual sense, at least. It was far too early to think of the physical sense of that word.

He wished he wouldn't think of her at all. In any sense. And he wished he knew why she was upset. He'd had three wives and three—or was it four?—concubines, and he'd never had this much trouble understanding their moods.

It occurred to him that he might call his old friend Alcuin, who still held the position of master teacher of the court, although he left more and more responsibility for the court school to Einhard.

Einhard would not do for a discussion on the subject of women. He was far too inexperienced. Only Alcuin would be wise enough to serve his needs. He spent a great amount of his time traveling to and from the many abbeys the king had bequeathed him, and as a result had gained experience in the ways of the world. Since he was expected at the Frankfurt council, he would, by now, be lodged in his home near the castle of Aix-la-Chapelle.

Charles would summon him. Now. Alcuin was used to that. In truth, the entire court was used to the king's bidding various of his confidants and officers to come to him at all hours of the night to discuss problems and issue orders. Everyone knew the king was a restless sleeper. What they didn't know was that the would-be nun was making him even more restless than usual.

Charles practiced his writing to pass the time while he waited in the outer room for Alcuin to arrive. He felt a growing dissatisfaction with his attempts. It seemed he could never master that art. Although he could recognize words easily enough when he was reading, he could never recall how the letters went together to construct the words. When he heard the door open and felt the cold night air rush in, he put his tablet and stylus aside and looked up to see the professor wrapped in otter skins, entering the room.

In spite of his reputation for great wisdom, he did not look old. His body was tall and straight, and his face showed only a few of the furrows time had plowed. His alert gray eyes made him look even younger. When he spoke, his voice was strong.

"My lord," he said as he bowed to the king. He appeared wide-awake, as if he, too, had not been sleeping.

"I am pleased that you are lodging in Aix-la-Chapelle at the moment," Charles said. "There is a matter I would discuss with you."

"Of course, Your Majesty." Alcuin seated himself in the chair the king indicated.

Charles was very keenly aware that it was the chair Amelia had sat in earlier. How could it be, he wondered, that she had sat in it only twice, and yet he had already come to think of it as her chair?

"You wish to discuss the veneration of images further in preparation for the Frankfurt council," Alcuin said, sounding confident and comfortable as he settled himself in the chair and accepted the cup of wine a servant handed him. He had been responsible for preparing a dossier on the matter of the veneration of images for the king to use at the meeting. "It is a sacrilege to call an image holy or to sprinkle it with incense," Alcuin said, taking up the discussion where they'd left off several days ago. "My lord, if you will, imagine a picture depicting the flight into Egypt. It could be either the Virgin or the ass who receives the incense." Alcuin, obviously pleased with his clever example, couldn't keep a smug little smile from his lips.

"I am well aware of your stand on the veneration of images." Charles could hear the sound of impatience in his own voice. Although he respected Alcuin's intelligence, he sometimes found him tiring, especially when he seemed all too pleased with himself. "I have another matter to discuss with you."

"Yes, my lord?" Alcuin leaned forward, eager to have the opportunity to display his wisdom further.

"It concerns . . ." Charles hesitated, clearing his throat. "It concerns women."

"Women?"

"Yes." Charles tried to force away his discomfort. After all, he was king. Nothing he said could be considered foolish. "They can be so . . . so difficult."

"The current law addresses that, my lord. It allows for the woman to prove her innocence in a crime with the trial by water." Alcuin spoke in his most pontificating voice. "The accused is thrown into the water with a heavy stone around her neck. If she floats she is innocent, but—"

"I know the law, and the law be damned! I am prepared to repeal that law," Charles shouted, losing patience. "No mortal, male or female, can float with a stone around the neck."

"Yes, Your Majesty." Alcuin slumped back slightly in his chair. "You are correct. The woman will drown unless the Lord God saves her because she is not guilty of—"

"I don't wish to talk about women drowning or not drowning," Charles said, causing Alcuin to recoil even further.

"Yes, Your Majesty." He looked as if he were trying to push himself through the back of the bearskin-covered chair.

"I want to discuss a particular woman. I . . . I don't seem to understand her in all cases."

"No, of course not, Your Majesty."

"What do you mean by 'of course not'?"

Alcuin opened his mouth, but no words emerged.

Charles continued. "It is my belief that since you have a measure of experience with women—wives, concubines, daughters—you might be able to help."

Alcuin's eyes brightened again. "Oh, yes. Certainly."

Charles rubbed his beard and looked at the fire. "I, of course, have wives, concubines, and daughters myself, but there is still one thing I don't understand about them."

"And what is that, my lord?"

"Their behavior."

Alcuin once again seemed incapable of speech. He stared at the king with his mouth slightly open.

"What does it mean?" Charles asked, leaning toward him slightly.

"I . . . I . . . uh . . ."

"A certain woman is upset with me about something. I can't for the life of me think what it is or what to do about it."

Alcuin released a great sigh of relief. "Oh," he said, smiling. "The remedy is quite simple. Give her jewels. Perhaps that necklace of lapis you brought back from Spain several years ago. It's still in your storehouse, isn't it?"

"No, no," Charles said as the frown on his face deepened. "Jewels wouldn't appeal to her. She's a nun."

"A nun, my lord?" Alcuin's face grew pale.

"Well, not yet, but she is preparing to be."

"I see."

"I must admit that I am attracted to her, and as long as she is not yet a nun . . ."

"I understand, my lord."

"Then what should I do?"

Alcuin's silence stretched for such a long time, Charles wondered if he was ill.

"Alcuin? What should I do?" Charles asked again.

"You must determine what it is she wants and give it to her." Alcuin's pomposity was reviving.

Charles frowned. "How does one go about determining what a woman wants?"

Alcuin's expression became grave. "You must keep this in mind, my lord. Woman, made from the rib of Adam to amuse him, is slighter of body and slighter of soul than man. She is, I would say, the lesser man. If her desires and thoughts seem incomprehensible, it is because God made her incapable of knowing them herself. You must not rush to give her what she wants too quickly, for she will change her mind. That is what I meant when I said to determine what she wants. You can do that one of two ways. The first is to wait until she tells you. That can lead to misfortune, because, as I said, she is never sure of what she wants. The second is to determine what you think she should want. Being of weaker mind, she will eventually be convinced that you are right."

When Alcuin finished with his advice, Charles sat looking at him for a long time, astounded. Finally he spoke. "Thank you, Alcuin. You may go to bed now."

Alcuin stood, bowed, and left with a self-satisfied smile on his face. Charles retired to his bedroom, wondering how a man who could understand arcane mathematics, rhetoric, and astrology, and who could reason theology and philosophy better than most, could be so pathetically ignorant of women.

He slept little for the remainder of the night, and he was up early to begin the preparations for his journey to Frankfurt. He felt no weariness for his lack of sleep, but all of the world appeared as an overgrowth of thorns, each one prepared to irritate him more than the last. Soldiers and servants were either too slow assembling provisions and securing them to horses, or else they were hasty and careless. To add to that, he expected all of his family at table to break their fast with him for the last time for a month or more, yet his wife and two of his daughters as well as two of his grandchildren had not been there. Bertha and her children claimed to have given in to watery noses, sneezing, and fever. Where was their fortitude? Fastrada claimed to be ill, too, and kept her youngest daughter at her side to nurse her. He had to admit she didn't appear well. Her face was swollen and had taken on a gray cast. He'd told her more than once that she should cut back on rich foods.

Amelia had not been there either, which was the biggest irritant of all. By this time she should have put aside whatever petty matter upset her the night before. Now he would have to go to the trouble of sending for her and waiting for her to appear so he could tell her he was leaving for the council meeting and that he would very likely have to leave from his Frankfurt palace to attack the Saxons, who were misbehaving again. Since he would be gone for such an extended length of time, he would tell her she was free to return to the abbey.

Soldiers waited patiently next to their mounts for the king to join them and give the signal that they could leave. Charles, in the meantime, waited in the throne room of the palace with considerably less patience. His fingers beat an irregular rhythm on the cold stone arm of his throne while a scowl puckered his forehead and pulled at his face. He was angry with her for taking so long to report to him. What could she possibly be doing? Nuns didn't spend time arranging their hair or adorning themselves with jewels or perfumes or robes with complicated fastenings. He was certain she would claim she'd been praying or reading scripture or attending to some other pious duty, when in reality she was simply trying to irritate him.

He watched the entryway to the throne room, prepared to rebuke her for her actions and to remind her of her duty to her king. When she appeared with the servant who had been sent to fetch her, he straightened in his chair and drew in his breath to blast her with his reprimand. Her face brightened with a shy smile as soon as she saw him, and his breath, rather than fueling a bombastic rebuke, escaped in a slow exhale.

She was dressed in her usual white robe and veil that was the mark of her novitiate, but it seemed to appear even whiter this morning, perhaps even to glow. Was it the smile on her face, small and shy as it was, that brightened everything? Made her eyes more luminous? And her face more beautiful?

Why was she smiling at all? Hadn't she been peeved about something the night before? Why was she being so damnably illogical? Was it any wonder that he sometimes sought relief in doing battle? At least a man could count on the enemy to be constant and cogent.

"Amelia," he said, since it was his right and duty to speak first, and he wanted to get this over with.

"Your Majesty," she replied with a little bow. "Allow me to say that I am happy for the opportunity to see you again before you leave."

"Yes, well, I thought it important that I remind you that I shall be gone for a long time." He spoke rapidly, trying to overcome the fact that the sight of her and the sound of her voice had thrown him off balance. "And," he added, "to tell you that you are free to leave—"

"Thank you, my lord," she said, interrupting him before he was finished. He had wanted to tell her that he reserved the right to call her back at his discretion, but she kept talking. "You are most gracious and generous with me," she said. "You have allowed me to learn from your steward lessons that will be invaluable to improving farming at Münster-Bilzen, and I—"

"You are fond of your home at Münster-Bilzen," he said, taking the opportunity to interrupt her, still with an eye toward keeping himself composed. "Both you and the abbey are deserving, and I wanted to tell you before you leave that I have decided to grant you the books you require for your library. I will summon a scribe to copy whatever you desire from my personal library. I have also decided to grant you timber from the royal forests for repair of the church."

"Thank you, my lord."

There was something more she wanted to say, Charles was certain, but she seemed to be having a difficult time forming the words.

"Are you feeling well?" he asked. The words sounded awkward even to his own ears.

"Oh, yes, Your Majesty. Quite well. It's just that I—"

"There seem to be others in the court who are suffering maladies," he said. "If you've caught something yourself, then by all means feel free to stay until you've recovered."

"As I said, Your Majesty, I am quite well, but I do wish to apologize to you for my behavior last night."

She had caught him off guard, and for a moment he couldn't think of what he should say. Then when he did speak, it seemed lame to him. All he could manage was, "Apologize?"

"I am afraid that I succumbed to the sin of covetousness," she said.

"Covetousness?" He'd done it again—stupidly replied to her with a one-word question.

"I ask God as well as you to forgive me."

"Of course," he said, although he had no idea what she had coveted and what that had to do with her behavior the night before.

"I ask your forgiveness for allowing my anger to show because you have promised my abbey to your daughter," she said. "I accept that it is your God-given right as well as God's will. Perhaps it is that God needed to teach me a lesson in humility. Nevertheless, I repent, and I ask your forgiveness."

The abbey! So that was it. He had all but forgotten that he'd promised it to Bertha. Now, of course, he remembered Amelia giving him her opinion that there should be no secular abbots or abbesses, and he remembered her ambition as well. He must have given her the impression that she would have her wish. He had no doubt that, in spite of her sincere attempt at repentance, she still desired—or as she put it, coveted—the abbey. If he granted it to her, though, she would surely go through with her plan to become a nun. There had to be something better in store for her, he thought. But was he really thinking of her benefit or his own? Did he simply want her to be more accessible to him? There was no time to dwell on that. The bishops were gathering at Frankfurt and the Saxons were spoiling for war.

"Amelia, my dear," he said, rising from his throne and placing his hand upon her head, "you are indeed a wise woman, and I assure you God and I both will forgive you for coveting something you cannot have."

10

MÜNSTER-BILZEN ABBEY

SPRING–AUTUMN 794

Amelia

A king is, by nature of his position, arrogant, but what right did he have to tell me whether or not God would forgive me? He was not my priest or confessor. And I suppose he thought he was being magnanimous by telling me *he* forgave *me*. Indeed! He should be the one asking *my* forgiveness.

All of those angry thoughts roiled inside me in spite of my continuing prayers for God to make me humble. I was further agitated by the questions the other nuns and novices threw at me. Their curiosity was even greater and more annoying than it had been earlier, when they first learned I'd been summoned to the palace.

Gertrude saw me shortly after I arrived with Einhard late on the second day after we left the palace. Before I was even in my cell, she stopped me.

"I see you have returned, Sister, after many days and nights traveling alone with the king's man."

"What you see is true, Sister," I said. "I have indeed returned."

She gave me a sour look. "Some would question the wisdom of a man and a maid alone on a journey."

"Really? I cannot think why."

After a little snort, she said, "You know of what I speak. You know the ways of the flesh."

"The ways of the flesh? I . . . I'm afraid I don't know what you mean. Would you explain it for me, the ways of the flesh?"

She opened her mouth to speak, but she could only sputter and give me an angry look before she hurried away.

That night at supper, I was less successful at stemming the flood of whispered questions. "Yes," I said, "it was just as I had been told. The king wished to consult me about a family matter. His son who had betrayed him. Yes, I gave the advice he requested. I suggested a monastery, because it would be banishment without extreme cruelty. No, I have no idea why he thought my advice worthy. Yes, the journey was fraught with dangers. Fierce beasts and brigands who tried to take our lives, but God gave me the strength of two men to overcome them."

I pray that God will forgive me for that exaggeration, since I uttered it only as an attempt to make them stop asking questions. Unfortunately, it didn't work. I still had to assure them that my conversations with the king were mostly about religious and philosophical matters or else about his family. I had to assure them as well that I saw no concubines, that I did not sleep in the palace but had my own room, so I could observe the rule of hours.

I grew weary of their thinly veiled suggestions that the king had wanted me for immoral purposes. That only added to my disgruntled feeling.

Apparently I wasn't doing as good a job concealing my emotions as I thought. Mother Landrada saw through me. That was apparent when she sent for me one day not long after I returned from Aix-la-Chapelle, and the king had gone off to his council meeting at Frankfurt.

"Something is troubling you, my child." She spoke in that odd way she had of sounding both compassionate and accusatory at the same time. "No, don't deny it," she said when she saw that I was about to. "I can see the anger in your lack of patience with others, not to mention the grim expression that has come to mar your face of late. Perhaps it is because you were asked to return to Münster-Bilzen when you would have preferred to remain at the palace."

"Oh, no! Quite the contrary. I am most happy to be home again." I spoke with perhaps a bit too much enthusiasm, because Mother Landrada gave me a look of suspicion. "It was an arduous journey, of course," I added. "And I did find that man called Einhard tiring."

Mother Landrada still had that odd look on her face. I was speaking the truth, however. I truly was glad to be back at the abbey, and I did find Einhard trying. Could she see that in spite of my anger with the king, I missed being with him? If she did, then she would know that it was not a fitting emotion for a woman who was about to take her vows of chastity and service.

Her gaze was locked on mine, and a little frown dug itself into her forehead. "Tell me about your visit to the palace," she said. "Tell me everything." Her look, her voice, reminded me of dark clouds gathering. I wasn't certain whether it was to be a storm of criticism or the gentle rain of compassion she harbored.

I was silent for a moment before I finally began to tell her what I had heard about the king promising Münster-Bilzen to his daughter, and how I had coveted it for myself. I also told her that he made me angry by suggesting that he knew whether or not God would forgive me. I had already told her, of course, of his promise to allow us access to any and all of the books in his library, and of his offer of timber from his forest, but I reminded her of those promises again, as well as the fact that he allowed me to learn farming techniques from his steward and to share some of my own with him. I didn't mention how much I enjoyed my long talks with the king or the way we laughed together or how much I wanted him to kiss me when I thought he was about to.

"I acknowledge his generosity. However, not only did I resent his implying that he knew whether or not God would forgive me for my covetousness, but I felt there were other things we should have discussed had he not been so eager to depart," I said, concluding my report.

"You have no right to resent his departure," Mother Landrada said. "You know it is his duty as king to attend the Frankfurt council. There will be important decisions made there for the Church. For all of the kingdom."

"I don't resent his royal duties," I said. "But following the council, he will leave for war."

"A necessary evil sometimes. It is for our protection."

"Is it?" I said. "Or is it greed? Is it that he simply wants to expand his realm?"

"And if he does, you will benefit as well. The richer and more powerful the kingdom, the safer we all are." Mother Landrada's voice had become scolding.

"He will do battle with the Saxons again." I couldn't keep the anger from my voice. "He says they are unruly. That they still prefer their pagan gods and to rule themselves." I watched Mother's face after I spoke. She was Saxon. The king and his army would be killing her own people, and I knew how it troubled her when the king fought past wars with them.

Mother erased the frown from her face and replaced it with a wistful expression. "It is true, the Saxons are slow to accept the true faith," she said. "But the Lord our God is patient. They will see the truth and accept Him."

"The king is less patient. He punishes them with death when they refuse baptism," I said. "I should think that would be enough to make them at least give lip service to the faith."

Mother Landrada sighed. "That is the way with kings.

One must believe that the true faith will triumph in its own way."

I couldn't help remembering that it was Mother Landrada herself who first told me of the ancient sprites and gnomes and undines who were the gods of woods, caverns, and rivers. She told the stories as children's tales to amuse me. I remembered in particular the story of the forest goddess who sometimes had the ears of a hare. She was called Eostre, Mother said, and her festival was held at dawn to celebrate the spring equinox. She said our festival of Easter is named in remembrance of her. "She is gone now, and another, the one true God, has taken her place," she said.

It was then that she would lapse into the story of the Vala, the far-seeing woman of her countrymen's legends, who predicted the end of the old gods and the coming of the great all-seeing God whose laws would last forever. He had come, she said, in the form of Our Lord Jesus the Christ.

Sometimes I wondered if the old gods were truly gone, since peasants still paid homage to them at the risk of severe punishment. Perhaps I, too, could be put to death for wondering, and Mother put to death as well for telling me the old stories she said she no longer believed.

"You are remembering, perhaps, that I myself was once a follower of the pagan gods," Mother said. It wasn't the first time she appeared to be able to read my thoughts.

"Yes, Mother," I replied. "I remember well the stories you told me about the old gods."

"The Lord God has, in his wisdom, placed many mysteries

in our midst." Mother Landrada looked away into the distance, as if she were seeing those mysteries. "One of them is that He did not make Himself known to all of mankind at once. Rather, He arranged it so that a few would have the truth and they would preach it to others. Those of us who were chosen last were forced to search for the One True God in our own way for a time. In those times the One True God presented Himself to us in many forms; that is to say, in the form of undines or sprites or gnomes, or in the form of Eostre or Woden. He did that in the same spirit in which we tell stories of fairies and magical happenings to children so they will understand certain small things until they are ready for the larger things."

"But would you have those children hanged who are not ready to grasp the truth of larger things? Would God have them hanged?"

At first I thought, judging by Mother Landrada's expression, that she was angry because I had been impertinent, but when she spoke, I realized it was not anger that marred her face but sadness.

"No, I would not hang them," she said. "Perhaps God, being male, would, just as the king does. But I am neither king nor God nor male. I am, instead, woman."

Charles had used similar words to justify his actions. "I am king," he had said, knowing that was all the justification he needed. Perhaps I should have told him some of the stories about the old gods Mother Landrada had told me. I could imagine how he might scold me for speaking of pagan gods and for suggesting they might not be truly dead because we borrowed their festivals for our own Christian celebrations. But might he not also laugh? The same way we both laughed when I forced him to admit the truth about why he didn't allow his daughters to marry? "We see both the light and the dark of each other's souls," he once said to me, "because our souls have mingled."

"Amelia?"

The sound of Mother Landrada's voice brought my attention back to the present. I looked at her and saw once again that ancient knowing in her eyes.

"Yes, Mother." My voice was not as steady as I might have wished.

"The matters you say should have been discussed by you and His Majesty, they were perhaps personal matters?"

"Personal, Mother?"

"You wish a more . . ." She hesitated but never took her eyes off of mine. "A more intimate way to serve the king?"

I felt my face grow warm, and I bowed my head for a moment, partly because I didn't want Mother to see my flush and partly because I needed time to collect my thoughts. "My wish," I said, raising my eyes to meet hers, "is to serve God and the Church. I wish for no more than to be a bride of Christ."

What I said was true, because I remembered in that moment what I always knew: No matter what my feelings for Charles, he was married to another. Beyond that, I had long ago made my decision and given my promise to live my life in service to God, a promise it would be wrong to break. I could be neither his wife nor his concubine.

"If you are not certain, you must tell me now. God does not want less than your whole heart."

"I am certain," I said, because I knew there was no other possibility.

When she dismissed me I went immediately to the fields, where the peasants attached to the abbey had already begun strewing the seeds for wheat and oats. I took my own sack and worked with them until time for evening prayers. It was the best method I knew to keep from thinking of Charles and other matters that had no place in the thoughts of a nun.

As spring warmed and became summer, I continued to work in the fields. When the grain sprouted, I helped the workers erect the wooden barriers to keep out hares and deer and other creatures. I taught the workers how to till the fields to be left fallow for crop rotation, the way the king's steward and I had discussed. I worked in the vegetable garden, and when that work was done I spent as much time in the library as I could before time for prayers. My work and study could no longer be directed toward the goal of becoming abbess, but I could not abandon either my books or my interest in agriculture and architecture, since I had by now become attracted to learning for its own sake.

In this way I passed the summer, trying not to think of Charles or of the fact that I would never be abbess. Instead, I would think only of making myself worthy of God's mercies and of asking his forgiveness for my many sins of pride and covetousness. I would fast and pray and work.

Mother Landrada became alarmed at my appearance. "The flesh has fallen from your bones, and you are too pale, except where darkness has settled around your eyes," she said. "Eat a little more. Don't spend such long hours in the fields or bent over books in the library."

"You advise me not to fast? Not to punish myself for my sins?" Hunger and fatigue made me feel cross and angry, and that was reflected in the sound of my voice when I spoke to her.

"God will punish when he sees fit," she said. "It is not your responsibility to punish yourself. Extreme penitence is the worst form of pride and vanity."

"My penitence is not extreme compared to others who flagellate or otherwise mutilate their bodies. I am unworthy even in that respect," I answered.

"Oh, my child," she said, shaking her head. "It is impossible to instruct someone whose mind is closed."

Her words surprised me. I hadn't thought of my mind as closed. Now it seemed that she didn't understand me at all. "I don't wish to appear disobedient to you, Mother," I said, hoping to make her see my plight. "It is only that I—"

"It is only that you are miserable," she said, interrupting me.

"Miserable? If I am miserable it is because of my sins."

"You are miserable because your lover has gone and

because you have lost the abbey." Her voice was stern with a hint of impatience.

I was both shocked and angry at what she said. "The king is not my lover."

"Ah, but you knew of whom I spoke. That is half the confirmation that I'm right."

I bowed my head, too embarrassed to look at her. "I have done nothing improper with the king." I spoke almost in a whisper.

"That is my point. You have done nothing improper."

I started to protest, but I said nothing, because it seemed that every time I spoke I showed myself a fool.

"It is not always easy to accept what befalls us," she said. "It is especially not easy for the young, who have not much experience with disappointment."

By now I was sinking deeper and deeper into the dark abyss of embarrassment. Mother Landrada must have thought I was acting like a spoiled child.

"Sometimes," she continued, "the best remedy is to separate ourselves from our old surroundings and go to a place where there are new challenges."

I felt as if my soul had just been snatched from me. She was sending me away! "Oh, no, Mother! Please don't—"

"I am not banishing you from the abbey," she said. "I love you like a daughter. I could not bear to do such a thing."

"Then what . . . ?"

"I would send you on a mission. It will be a journey of

several days to the village of Temsche on the River Scheldt. A bishop, Gerold of Dorested, who stopped by here while you were yet at the palace in Aix-la-Chapelle, told me of the great need of the people there. Many are pagan and know not the way of Our Lord Jesus Christ, but beyond that, they are starving. Bishop Gerold says their farms are poor and their harvest light, even in good years. You could teach them, Amelia. Teach them all that you have taught yourself, and they will not go hungry. Perhaps it will also help you decide if you are truly meant to enter into the monastic life."

She had thrown me a morsel. I grasped it like the hungry and empty soul I had become.

II

The Road to Temsche
Autumn 794

Amelia

Preparations for the journey were not complicated. I would take along enough bread and cheese for one day and expect to depend upon the charity of others or my own skill for the remaining days of my journey. I would take a warm cloak, since the winds of autumn had already sung the first song of summer's death and would no doubt be in full chorus as I journeyed north. I would also take a letter of introduction from Mother Landrada.

"You will follow the road through the forest," she said, "and by the end of the day, according to Bishop Gerold, you will see the abbey of Uslar, a small abbey. Spend the night there, and the next morning the monks will show you the road to follow to Temsche. The bishop says you will be there after another day's journey." I was to present the letter of introduction to the abbot of Uslar.

She insisted that one of the abbey's servants, a man named Grimoald who was strong and heavily built and of a good and pious nature, accompany me. I saw no need for his company, but Mother refused to consider my thoughts on the matter. However, as God would have it, Grimoald fell ill at the last minute with a sickness that was sweeping the monastery—a fever and a raspy cough—so Adolpha volunteered to go with me. Mother was not entirely pleased with that arrangement.

"It is not seemly for women to travel alone," she said. "There is the impropriety and there is the danger. I can only pray that your being women of the church will protect you."

I assured her that, since the journey was to be short along a well-traveled route, there likely would be little opportunity for an evil person to do us harm without being seen. Still, she insisted that we wait until Grimoald's cold-weather sickness passed. My next argument was that a delay of uncertain duration would not serve the mission well. At last she gave in, although I would be hard-pressed to repeat exactly what I said that influenced her. Perhaps it was only that my obstinacy wore on her until she relented.

Our journey began as all long journeys inevitably begin—early in the morning. The air was the color of lavender and had the cool, crisp feel of dying leaves. We walked away from the abbey headed northwest and soon entered a cold, dark forest where the air lost its crispness and became as soggy as the carpet of fallen leaves that covered the forest floor. Before long a little moisture began to fall in a slow, steady drizzle that deceived us by making us believe such a small amount of rain could not possibly make us uncomfortable. By noon, however, it had soaked through our cloaks and our hoods and wimples and flattened our shorn hair against our skulls. My cloak felt like a weight of lead on my shoulders. Other travelers we met along the way appeared equally miserable.

We continued for several hours, stopping only twice to relieve the pressure of our bladders before we slogged onward in the ever-increasing rain. We had spoken very little to each other during the miserable day's journey, which ended at nightfall, not at the monastery Mother Landrada said we would find at the edge of the forest, but at a damp and dark cave that offered us the only protection we could see.

I shivered with cold as I gathered twigs and logs to start a fire, but Adolpha fairly trembled. Her hands were too stiff with the cold to be of much help in gathering fuel.

"Remove that damp cloak," I said as I struck the flint I had brought along. "I'll have a fire shortly."

"I am so cold, so very cold," she said, her voice trembling as much as her body.

"Eat a little of this," I said, offering her the bread and cheese we'd brought. She accepted it, and I went back to trying to get the fire burning. It took much longer than I had hoped, since the wood was wet. For a long time we had nothing but smoke, which set us both to coughing. Finally, I summoned the courage to walk farther back into the dark cave, where I found a few dry pieces of wood. By the time I had a meager fire going, Adolpha had eaten no more than a few bites of the food, and she was still shivering and coughing. Obviously she had the cold-weather malady that had swept our abbey.

After I'd spread our cloaks on the ground next to the fire, I took her in my arms and held her, trying to warm her.

"You're cold, too," she said when she sensed my own shivering.

"Hush. We'll both be warm soon."

"The fire is going out," she said. "What will happen to us? Will we die of the cold? Will we be eaten by wild animals?"

"We won't die. The temperature is not cold enough this early in the year to freeze water or a person's blood. And if the fire goes out, God will protect us." I spoke those words with no confidence. I was by no means certain God was willing to protect us against wild animals or the gnawing cold dampness.

"A person can never be sure of that," Adolpha said, obviously sharing my feelings.

"We must have faith," I forced myself to say.

"But God often seems so capricious."

There was a long silence before I finally responded. "Yes," I said. "He does, doesn't He?"

"My mother, my own mother, though she professed to be Christian, still believed in the forest goddess." Adolpha, who was still shaking from the cold, whispered those words as if she might be afraid God or one of His clerics would hear her. "My mother said the goddess protects those she favors."

"Perhaps she will favor us." I knew I should never have spoken those words, or that I should have at least made the sign of the cross when I did speak. I made no sign, however. My hands were busy rubbing the flesh on Adolpha's fore-arms as I tried to warm her.

"It is evil for us to be talking like this," she whispered.

"Then we must cease the talk," I said, knowing she was right.

Adolpha was quiet for a while, and she even slept a little, though it was a fitful sleep. I slept poorly as well, especially after the fire burned out and I was unable to find more wood. I was even wider awake when I saw the red eyes of some four-legged beast staring at me from just outside the mouth of the cave. Finally, though, the beast grew tired of us and moved away.

I ate a little more of the cheese the next morning, but Adolpha refused to eat anything at all, and, although the smoke from the damp wood had cleared from the cave, her cough lingered, and her voice, when she was able to speak at all, made the cracking sound of wood splitting.

We walked side by side through the fog and mist the forest had made out of the rain and the morning. Adolpha leaned heavily on me as we wound our way across the wooded plain that was interrupted by treacherous ravines. At least the rain had stopped, replaced by dark clouds as heavy and soggy as our cloaks.

Adolpha still was unwilling to eat more than a bite or two throughout the day, and as the light waned and the rain started again, her cough worsened. It seemed a great blessing when, well before dark, I saw the outline of what I took to be an abbey ahead of us. It had taken us a full day longer to reach it than the bishop had led Mother Landrada to believe.

From a distance, I could see the abbey was indeed small compared to Münster-Bilzen and was no more than a collection of wooden huts with thatched roofs. The church was recognizable only by a crude cross on the top of one of the huts. Spindly logs bound together with rawhide strips formed the cross. The settlement of houses and shops that inevitably sprouts around a monastery was small and poor as well.

A monk, standing at the gate to the abbey, watched us for a long time as we approached, and continued to watch us, mute as a stone, when we stopped in front of him.

"Greetings, Brother," I said as I approached him.

He responded with no more than a slight nod.

"We come from Münster-Bilzen Abbey, east and south of here. We are on our way to serve the people of Temsche on the River Scheldt."

He gave us another little nod and turned away, walking

into the abbey grounds. I assumed, or at least hoped, that he meant for us to follow, so I walked behind him, leading Adolpha.

The monk stopped in front of another monk, who wrestled with a squealing sow. He was trying to pull her by the rope around her neck into one of the huts. The monk who had led us inside the gates spoke in a low voice to the second monk, then bowed and walked away.

The second monk's robe was soiled with the filth of the pigpen, and his beard and hair were a mass of tangled brambles. He was having a hard time holding the rope that held the pig, but that didn't keep him from scrutinizing us for several seconds before he spoke. "Women traveling alone. And women of the church at that."

"If we may see the abbot, please," I said. "We have a letter of introduction from our abbess." Since Adolpha was a full-fledged nun and I only a novice, it should have been she who spoke. The sickness was making her too miserable to utter a word, however, and I was beginning to suspect that she burned with fever.

"We have little to share," the monk said.

"We require little," I answered. "Shelter from the rain. A cup of hot milk for my sister."

He ignored my request. "What abbey would send two women out alone?"

"If we may see your abbot, please." My growing impatience was evident in my voice.

"You speak with him now." He gave the pig a hard

kick, which made the pig squeal even louder. "I am Abbot Hincmar."

For a moment, I was too stunned to respond. Finally, I took the letter of introduction from the pouch I wore at my waist and handed it to him. He took it, examined it front and back, and handed it back to me. It was obvious that he was not able to read it.

"We'll share what we have," he said. "But all who come here must work for their keep." He glanced at Adolpha, who slumped against me. "If she's not able, then you will do the work of two."

"If those are your rules, then of course, I . . ."

The abbot turned and walked away before I was able to finish voicing my agreement. He looked back over his shoulder and motioned with his hand that we should follow. I did, walking a few feet behind the angry pig while I held on to Adolpha.

The abbot stopped in front of a small structure with a thatched roof. There was one window and a door. The shutter was missing on the window. "You will sleep here," he said. "I'll send blankets after you do the milking. Two goats and a cow." He pointed to a patch of grass where the animals grazed. "There," he said. "Dagobert will bring a pail."

Up to this point, Adolpha had made no noise at all except to cough and sneeze. "It looks dirty," she said, looking at the little hut.

The abbot looked at her and laughed, showing rotting teeth and several gaps where teeth were missing. "You are used to luxury in your abbey, are you? We are a poor cloister. Our crops barely feed us, and some of our group die each year of starvation. We have no vineyards, no wheat for extra bread to sell for a profit, no gold in our coffers. Only a small brewery. None of the king's rich friends are fighting over Uslar Abbey. No one is trying to grab my office. I shall be abbot forever." He laughed again and walked away, leading his pig.

"Come, Adolpha," I said. "The hut will serve us fine. It's no dirtier than the cave."

"Yes, it is!" She might have said more, but a paroxysm of coughing seized her, and she was unable to speak. Even breathing required a supreme effort from her, it seemed.

After a considerable struggle, I was able to get her into the hut. It had an earthy smell emanating from the hard-packed dirt floor. There were no furnishings, not even a table or a chair. The best I could do was prop Adolpha in a corner of the room and wrap her still-damp cloak around her. By the time I accomplished that, the monk the abbot had called Dagobert, the same monk who had met us at the gate, came to the door with a wooden pail.

"Take the milk there," he said, pointing to one of the crude buildings. I assumed it served as the refectory.

It had been several years since I'd had to be a milkmaid at Münster-Bilzen, and I had lost some of my proficiency. It took me an unusually long time to rid all three of the animals of their milk. I took it, one pail at a time, to the refectory, where the abbot and his nine monks were already dining on hard bread and cheese. Some of the men grabbed the pail as soon as I entered and dunked their bread in the milk to soften it. Another snatched the pail away and, turning it up to his mouth, drank greedily. The same thing happened with the second pail. When I had milked the last goat, I stopped by the hut assigned to Adolpha and me and helped Adolpha drink some of the warm milk from the pail. She would have no more than a swallow, but I took the opportunity to drink some myself. When I arrived at the refectory this time, no one was there, so I took the remaining milk and the few crusts of bread I could find scattered on the table back to our hut.

The blankets had arrived while I was gone. They were coarsely woven, and a sizable colony of bedbugs had taken up lodging in the rough threads. We bedded down, huddled together on the earthen floor with the colonized blankets spread over us. Adolpha's cough kept both of us from enjoying a sound sleep. Her body grew so hot she threw the blanket aside.

"I can't sleep. It's so hot." Her voice was hoarse.

"It's the fever," I said.

"I can't sleep," she said again. "Talk to me, please." In spite of her complaint of heat, she was shivering.

"It's late, Adolpha, and I'm tired after a day of walking and milking."

Adolpha made no reply, but within a few moments I heard her sniffling.

"What's wrong now, Adolpha?" I sat up and pulled my

blanket tight around my shoulders. I could feel its inhabitants nibbling at my flesh.

"I . . . I'm afraid," Adolpha whispered. She wiped her eyes with the backs of her hands.

"God will protect us." I spoke in a whisper also. Neither of us wanted the inhabitants of the abbey to hear us.

"I'm so sick I feel as if I might die," she said.

I reached a hand out to touch her. "You won't die, Adolpha. You have the cold-weather sickness. You know it doesn't last forever."

"Sometimes it does."

"Why are you so gloomy?" I asked. "It's not like you. And anyway, I'll take care of you. Just as you took care of me when all the nuns and novices were pestering me about what immoral acts I might have witnessed or even indulged in while I was at the palace."

I whispered those words hoping they would make her laugh. She didn't laugh, and her response surprised me. "You love him, don't you, Amelia?"

"Love him? Who?"

"You know who," she said in her hoarse voice. "The king."

"The king? Oh, of course I do. Everyone in the kingdom loves—"

"You know what I mean, Amelia. Stop pretending you don't."

Only a mist of pale moonlight entered the little hut through the open window, but it was enough for me to see that Adolpha's serious gaze was locked on my face.

"I . . . I don't know," I whispered. "Sometimes I'm afraid I do."

"A person shouldn't be afraid of love," she said.

"I will soon be a bride of Christ. I shouldn't be—"

"I hope you *are* in love with him, Amelia. I think to love someone in that manner must be a wonderful thing. I wish it could happen to me as well."

"Adolpha! If Mother Landrada could hear you say that, she would—"

"I think she was in love once, too."

"Mother Landrada? Why do you say that?" I was both shocked and surprised at what she said.

"I think it's why she never took the veil. She didn't want to be a bride of Christ. She wanted to be a bride of her lover, and she does penance for feeling that way by not using the profits from the abbey the king granted her for her own comfort, the way others do. She pays it all back to God."

"But who?" I was even more shocked. "Whom did she love?"

"I don't know, but I'm certain their love was more beautiful than . . ." A racking cough interrupted her, and she trembled even more. "I'm so cold, Amelia," she said and moved closer to me.

She alternated between chills and fever for most of the night, making us both sleep only fitfully.

Just before daybreak, Dagobert walked into the hut without knocking or announcing himself first. I was bent over Adolpha, trying to wipe her brow with a corner of the filthy blanket.

"Ah, there it is." He pointed to the wooden pail that sat next to our crude pallets. "You should have brought it back to the refectory. When you finish the morning milking, make sure you leave it there before you continue your journey." He paused a moment before he spoke again, and pointed to Adolpha. "What's wrong with that one?"

"She has the cold-weather sickness," I said.

"More than that, I would say." He walked to her pallet and squatted beside her, then bent over to place his ear to her chest. "A flux in the lungs," he said, raising his head to look at me. "And she burns with fever. Has she spat out blood or pus?"

"I'm not sure," I said and sniffed. My nose had become watery, and my throat felt as if it were full of nettles.

"She will. Soon enough." He looked at her for several seconds, then glanced around the room. "She needs more blankets. A pillow to prop her up. A fire to warm her. And herbs." He started for the door, speaking to me over his shoulder on his way out. "Go. Milk the cow and the goats. I'll see to the nun."

I was loath to leave Adolpha, yet I dared not disobey, lest the abbot force us out. At least the milking went a bit faster this time. By the time I returned to the hut with a little of the milk in the pail, the one room was smoky from a fire that burned in a small brazier Dagobert had set next to the window to allow some of the smoke to escape. At least the room was warmer. He had removed Adolpha's damp cloak and wrapped her in two blankets equally as dirty as the first two he had brought. He held a steaming cup to her lips and was trying to force her to drink.

"I brought her some milk," I said and sneezed.

"She won't take it." He spoke without looking at me until I sneezed a second time. "You will drink some of this." He shoved the steaming cup toward me and held it out until I took it. "Drink," he said.

I took a sip, and my mouth was immediately assaulted with a putrid bitterness. It was not unexpected, since I, myself, had used and administered tea made of a fetid secretion from certain plants of the forest. Nevertheless, it made me gag.

"The nun is too sick for a journey," Dagobert said, taking the cup from me. "She must rest here for a few days. As for you, if there is no fever, you can leave if you must."

"I'll stay until she's well enough to accompany me," I said.

I half expected him to tell me to leave anyway, since there were not sufficient provisions to feed me. He said nothing. Instead he gave me an odd look punctuated with a troubled frown and left the hut.

For three days I continued to drink the vile concoction administered by Dagobert. My nose ceased to drip and my sneezing stopped.

Adolpha died on the third day.

12

Saxony

Autumn–Winter, 794–795

Charles

Charles could sense the weariness of his favorite mount, Zephyrus, but he knew the horse possessed great heart and would stand until the battle was won. Charles was tired as well. The drawn-out battle against the Saxons had taken its toll, both in soldiers and in stamina. But this would be the final battle before winter sent both his Frankish troops and the Saxons home.

The king's hope now was to mount a flank attack. He had moved some of his foot units closer to the center of the battlefield and kept some in force on the left flank of the enemy, along with a few mounted troops, while he and the other mounted men were moving to the right flank. If he could launch an overpowering attack on the weaker flank of the

Saxons, he could destroy them. That would force the Saxons back against the River Weser.

Charles sat Zephyrus in the front line of the cavalry. The men on either side of him were his best troops, noblemen who supplied their own horses and weapons and who fought for the king but also for the land and livestock they would receive as reward for their service. With his lance raised, the king shouted the command.

"Attack!"

Charles felt his mount's muscles bunch and then stretch as Zephyrus lunged ahead, his strong, powerful body moving with as much vigor as the furious west wind that inspired his name. The king's soldiers raced ahead on their mounts, their long lances atilt and ready. Charles struck the first blow, knocking a Saxon from his horse, then spearing him between his eyes and through his skull with the iron tip of the lance. The Saxon's blood gushed out, masking his face and turning his sun-blond hair the color of rust. Charles pulled his lance from the soft tissue and hard bone of the man's head and swung the weapon in one fluid motion to unhorse another Saxon.

Men were falling all around him, and when he spurred Zephyrus on, the horse lifted his front legs and pushed off with his hind legs in a graceful jump over one of Charles's own fallen soldiers.

The Saxons were inferior horsemen compared to Charles's troops, but they were men born to the battle, fierce and strong-hearted. Dominating one flank didn't mean they were beaten. Charles knew full well that the enemy might be overwhelming him on the left. He'd given orders to a reserve unit waiting behind him to charge forward when the commander saw the need.

He had no sense of how long the battle raged, but he fought with a righteous and holy purpose. He would continue to fight until all of Saxony renounced their worship of devils and false gods and accepted the sacraments of the true faith.

What was it Amelia had said? She had reminded him that the Saxons had renounced their gods before, then gone back to them as soon as his back was turned. She'd also said torture was not the way to bring salvation to the enemy.

He felt a sudden blow and then a sharp pain in his right shoulder and knew even before he saw the blood running down his arm that he had to put all thoughts of Amelia from his mind. He pulled his sword with his left hand and in a quick movement lopped off the head of the foot soldier who had wounded him.

Anger coursed through him as red and hot as his blood. He was angry at the Saxons for refusing Christianity, at Amelia for invading his thoughts, and at himself for allowing it. It gave him the strength he needed to push on, to bathe himself in his enemy's blood, to slash heads and hearts and limbs until he and the mounted troops with him could cut into the center, where foot soldiers were as bloodied as he and where more bodies fell to his sword.

When the Saxons were finally backed against the river, he offered each man salvation and asked him to consent to baptism. If they refused, he showed them no mercy, slicing off their heads without giving them a chance to reconsider. He had no conception of how long the siege and massacre lasted, and by the time he reached his royal encampment, he had lost enough blood from his wounded shoulder that he was too weak to dismount without help.

Darkness followed. A long, hollow tunnel of darkness that filled him with anxiety. He moved through the tunnel barely able to breathe because of the invisible weight on his chest. He would surely die, he thought, until he heard the voice, far away, at the end of the tunnel.

The voice called his name.

"Charles. Charles. I am with you now."

"Amelia?" He wasn't certain that he spoke her name aloud.

"Yes," the voice said. "I am with you now."

"Where?" He tried to move toward the voice. "I can't see you." The weight on his chest increased, and he felt heat burning his life away.

"Breathe," she said. "Breathe, my love. I am with you now."

She stood in front of him in the light. Her arms were extended, and she was smiling. "Breathe, my love," she said again.

Later, when he awoke and found himself lying on a crude cot covered with animal skins, he remembered nothing at first, beyond seeing the Saxons with their backs to the river, their wild, wheat-colored hair and their coarse tunics blackened with blood. He had forgotten, even, his wound until he rolled to his side to lift himself off the cot and felt fingers of fire digging into his shoulder. He fell back, helpless, to the cot.

"I beg Your Majesty, stay!" Charles heard the voice and opened his eyes slowly to see a man he didn't recognize hovering over him.

"No. Can't stay," he said, remembering now. "Must find her again—"

"No need to find anyone. You've won the battle, Your Majesty. The Saxon chieftain has surrendered and offered his remaining troops for baptism." The man walked toward him, carrying a bowl of water and strips of coarse cloth.

"Baptism? Then I must—"

"The cleric you brought with us is baptizing the last of the devil-worshiping horde now, by the light of torches." The man gave him a gentle push, forcing him once again down to the cot. "The priest seems to have convinced them that the fires of hell will be worse than the icy waters of the Weser," he said, chuckling.

"Where is she?" he asked.

"Where is who, Your Majesty?"

"She was here, but now she . . ." His mind was drowning in a yellow haze, robbing him of clear thought. He had to sleep. Looking down at his shoulder, he saw bandages for the first time, saw how his blood had painted them crimson, saw the new bandages laid out to replace them. Then before he could comprehend it all, he lost consciousness. This time there was no darkness. There was light and the sense of her nearness.

On the second day, he bellowed for food. The man, the physician whose name he still didn't know, did his best to convince him that he should wait at least another day.

"Roasted venison!" Charles roared. "I will have it roasted on a spit over a slow-burning fire. While I wait for that, I will have whatever is in the store of supplies we brought. Beans and bread, if nothing else. And wine. Plenty of wine."

The physician bowed and backed away and immediately summoned a servant to see that the king's wishes were granted. He returned a short time later with the beans, bread, and wine, as well as a hare that had been caught that very morning and cooked in boiling oil.

Charles was out of bed and seated at a small table when the food arrived. He took it from the physician and immediately bit into the succulent flank of the hare. "Good," he said, wiping his mouth with his sleeve.

"The venison will be ready by nightfall," the man said.

"What's your name, physician?" Charles spoke around another morsel of the hare.

"I am called Arno, Your Majesty."

"You are Frankish?"

"I am pleased to call myself Frankish now, my lord, but I was born among the Lombards."

"Indeed," Charles said, thinking the Lombard was wise to call himself Frankish, since it had been twenty years since the Lombards had succumbed to his superior army.

"I have served your army faithfully for seven years, Your Majesty. Ever since the day you personally chose me as your physician."

"I chose you, you say?"

"Perhaps you don't remember me because you have never been seriously wounded until now," Arno said.

"I must have known then that you were exceptionally skilled." Charles moved his shoulder in circles and lifted his arm, feeling only a slight stiffness and minor pain.

"Thank you, Your Majesty."

"But you have much to learn," the king added and noted how the color drained from Arno's face. "You should know that starving a man is not the way to heal him." Charles covered his mouth with his hand in a futile attempt to hide a burp and then reached for the wine cup. "Food and wine," Charles said, raising the cup. "That is the way to heal a man. Remember that."

"I will, of course, remember that," Arno said, bowing low.

"Good. Now tell me, who has commanded the army while I was recuperating?"

"Your son, Charles the Younger. Quite ably, I might add. You have trained him well, Your Majesty."

The mention of his son immediately brought to mind the memory of Pepin, his eldest, who should have been in command, but who now spent his days in a monastery. It was Amelia who had prescribed his punishment. Amelia, whose touch, whose presence still lingered about him somewhere, just out of reach. Amelia, wise and capable enough to be queen. Had she been his wife, she would not have chided and criticized Pepin to the point of rebellion as Fastrada had. Had she been his wife, she would no doubt have found her royal duties of managing the kingdom while the king was gone sufficient to satisfy her desire to make good use of her mind. She would not need excessive education, as she thought she needed now. And she was beautiful, more beautiful than any of his wives or concubines. He liked to imagine her dressed in red silk as Himiltrude, his first concubine and mother of Pepin, had done.

"Your Majesty?"

The sound of Arno's voice brought him back to the present.

"Your Majesty, are you all right?"

"Quite all right," Charles said, grateful that Arno couldn't read his thoughts. "Here," he said, shoving the wine flask toward the physician. "Find your cup and join me." A smile played at his lips. Amelia invaded his thoughts again. She was indeed with him, and he knew she always would be.

He insisted on traveling the next day, despite objections from some of his officers, including his son. Arno, the physician, was afraid to protest. He had been found wrong in prescribing the king to fast. He wasn't inclined to show himself a fool again by going against the king's wishes.

"I'm weary of war and weary of military encampments," Charles said. "I was at Frankfurt for the meeting of the council for months, and I've been as many months at war with the Saxons. I crave the baths and the comforts of my newest palace at Aix," he said. He didn't mention that another reason for returning there was that of all his palaces scattered throughout his kingdom, the palace at Aix-la-Chapelle was the closest to Münster-Bilzen Abbey.

His son was among the first to object. "Winter has already set in, Father. A messenger from the fort of Antwerpen says the snow is already belly-deep on a horse at the Abbey Corvey."

Charles refused to give in, although he knew his son gave wise counsel. "When the snow is too deep to ride through, we'll ride around it, and we'll find lodging. No man in the kingdom, from the lowest peasant to the wealthiest bishop, would refuse lodging to the king and his men."

The army, with Charles in the lead, his shoulder bandaged and his arm in a sling, rode west along the River Weser, hoping by nightfall to reach Verden, where there was a bishopric. They camped ten miles from the king's goal. Horses as well as men were exhausted by their long, slow slog through fallen snow.

Heavy snows kept them in their camp for three days. On the fourth, they rode to Verden, where they were welcomed by the bishop and where Charles deemed it prudent to stay until spring. Though he would not admit it to anyone, lest he appear too weak to lead, his shoulder, after the original numbness, had become painful, and the wound still bled. What was worse, he could no longer sense Amelia's presence.

He grew weary of pretending cheerfulness and began to spend long hours alone in a darkened room while black clouds covered the world outside with snow. His officers worried about him, and the physician gave him herbs and tonics, but the black mood continued.

Much of his time in the darkness was spent thinking of Amelia. If only he could write better, he would send a letter to her at Münster-Bilzen with instructions to write him a response. He couldn't do that, however, for fear she would laugh at his lack of skill. He usually enlisted Einhard to write letters for him, but Einhard was back at Aix-la-Chapelle. It would be awkward to ask even Einhard to write such a letter as he wanted to write to Amelia. Besides that, even the best of his horsemen might not be able to make it through the heavy drifts that separated his camp from the abbey. And what would he say? That he would give her the abbey she so wanted? How could he do that when such a move would separate her from him forever? Could he tell her he wanted her to be his wife? Might she not balk at that, especially since he was married to Fastrada? Divorce would be awkward and difficult, especially since the papacy had become so much against it.

On the eve of the winter solstice, he decided to swallow his pride and attempt a letter, one with no other message than declaring his love for her. He sent a rider through the snow toward the abbey on the day of the solstice when, in spite of the darkness, the weather had cleared some.

When the month called Ostramanoth arrived, which is when the world reawakens and green shoots show themselves in the snow, the rider had not returned. By that time Charles had lost some of his girth as well as some of his vigor, and the shoulder still had not healed. Nevertheless, he commanded that he and his troops would begin the journey home.

They had crossed the River Weser and had come upon Nienburg when a messenger riding from the palace at Aix-la-Chapelle met them. It was not the one Charles had sent to Münster-Bilzen, but another, who had neither seen nor heard of the messenger the king had sent out earlier. This messenger had ridden from Regensburg. He brought with him the news that Queen Fastrada had died in her bed at the palace in Regensburg the day after the feast of the Nativity of Jesus Christ.

13

Uslar Abbey and Beyond

Autumn 794

Amelia

We buried Adolpha after a Christian Mass in a windswept plot forested with at least a dozen crude crosses of the same style that topped the church.

The cross on Adolpha's grave was no different—two sticks of wood bound together with leather strips to form the cross. There were no words etched in the wood to bear witness to her name. I knew that in all too short a time the wood would rot and the grave would become overgrown with grass. In future years and future centuries men and women would walk across the land or perhaps even build their structures there without knowing a remarkable woman lay beneath their feet.

It was with those thoughts and a heavy sadness that I left Uslar Abbey alone to make my way to Temsche. Abbot

Hincmar consented, with reluctance, to provide me with a loaf of hard bread and a little beer to take with me on my journey. With considerably less reluctance, he gave me directions, telling me how to find the old Roman road to Nevelles, where, at a crossroads, I would turn north to the fortress of Antwerpen and on to Temsche. I could expect to walk at least three days, he said.

"You will reach the village of Drest by nightfall. There's a church there. The priest, Father Stavelot, and his wife will welcome you." The abbot spoke with a kind of impatience that led me to believe he was eager for me to leave.

The road, though it was ancient, had been kept in good repair. I had heard praises for the king's attention to the roads many times from visitors to Münster-Bilzen, and now I saw for myself that the praise was well deserved. I supposed, however, that he kept the roads repaired in order to move his armies with expedience when he set out to conquer more people and land for church and kingdom. He was never far from my mind, if truth be told, although most of the time I wasn't thinking of his armies or his roads but of the way his arms had felt around me that night under the stars.

I tried not to think of him but to think of God and to thank him for the pleasant weather. I suffered little from cold, since I now had not only my own cloak, but Adolpha's as well. I believed, of course, that she was now in heaven with God and His angels, but I could not force away the thought of her lying in the cold ground, perhaps even shivering without her cloak. I'm certain it was Satan himself who put such thoughts into my mind. I managed to force him away by reciting psalms. I grew weary of the psalms, though, and the energy I expended trying not to think of Charles or of Adolpha made me tired. A great longing for something to read swept over me and plagued me until twilight, when I came upon the village of Drest.

A more welcome sight I cannot recall. I could see several buildings nestled together on the outside of the town's wall. In the dim light they reminded me of pups snuggled against their mother. The walls of the town appeared to be crumbling in places, as if it was too much trouble to mend them, since buildings were spilling out of them anyway. There were no lights to welcome me. I knew that what candles might be burning flickered behind doors and windows closed against the advancing autumn.

Fortunately for me the gates had not yet been closed, and I was able to walk beyond the wall along a dirt path. I could smell cooking fires burning and see smoke levitating from chimneys. The few people who had not yet returned to their home fires and were still on the street gave me curious glances. Some combined their stares with slight nods. One man even bothered to speak and to point out the obvious.

"The church is there, Sister." He pointed to a building on a small hill. "You'll find Father Stavelot and his wife inside."

I nodded my thanks and made my way to the church. It was built in the architectural style most common in the kingdom, with a long nave ending in a semicircular apse. It was as plain inside as it was outside. The floor was wooden planks, and the walls were decorated only with simple drawings on wood to represent the stations of the cross. The altar was equally as plain and held a tall wooden cross and a wooden bowl that I presumed held the Host.

I paid my respects to the Host with a bow and the sign of the cross and was about to leave, assuming the priest had left, when I heard a noise that made me turn to a door to my right. Someone was speaking behind that door. I could hear at least two voices.

When I knocked, the door opened, and I was greeted by a man in clerical robes. Behind him I saw a woman bending over a hearth and stirring a pot. She looked up when I spoke.

"Father Stavelot?"

"Yes?" He was a man in the middle years of his third decade, with thinning hair, a long, grim face, and not an ounce of fat on his bones.

"I am Amelia of Münster-Bilzen Abbey. I come with greetings from Abbot Hincmar of Uslar Abbey, whence I have recently come. He said I might expect a night's lodging with you."

"Hincmar of Uslar, you say." He spoke with a strong measure of scorn or disgust in his voice, and I think he might have been about to turn me away had his wife not intervened.

"Come in, Sister. Of course you will share our lodging

and our meal as well." Madam Stavelot walked toward me, wiping her hands on the skirt of her brown linen dress. She was a pleasant-looking woman with a round, flushed face, perhaps a few years younger than her husband. "We turn away no one, as Christ himself taught us. Certainly not a woman of the church."

She pulled me inside toward the hearth while her husband stood by with the frown on his face bubbling to a boil.

"Stavelot," she called to him over her shoulder. "Fetch the chair. The one with the down cushion. And you, Sister, off with your cloak. Both of them. And a fine weave they are, I see. I'll hang them here, on this hook. You'll warm yourself by the fire now."

In an amazingly short time, I was seated on the down cushion with my cloaks hanging nearby, while Madam Stavelot stirred a pot of what looked to be hearty stew. Her husband sat at the table reading the Bible aloud in a muffled voice. It was obvious reading was difficult for him. While he read, his wife stirred the stew and peppered the room with her chatter.

"A woman traveling on her own, you are! Not a common thing, I would say. People frown upon such a thing. For the wrong reasons, I say. How can they call it an immoral act when they know not the reason for the journey? Ah, the rules we women must follow! I say the problem lies with the clergy. Ignorant as they are, they yet have all the right to call whatever they will immoral. I should like to teach them a thing or two, I would. Think you they will listen? Hah! A fool knows the answer to that, I say. . . ."

She went on and on with her talk, making me wonder why her husband didn't protest her slander of the clergy. However, he only continued his struggle with the words of the text he tried to read, apparently oblivious to anything happening around him.

I did my best to give my attention to Madam Stavelot's words, but that proved to be as difficult for me as deciphering Latin was for the priest. All I could think of was how the thick stew with its savory aroma of mutton and onions would taste. Ambrosial, I thought, as water gathered in my mouth in anticipation. I had long since eaten the last of the abbey's bread, which remained hard and dry even when I soaked it in beer.

"The food which the Lord has provided us," Madam Stavelot said as she placed a large bowl filled with the stew in the center of the table where the priest sat. The bowl sent an ethereal stream of incense up in a sensuous curl toward the ceiling. That got Father Stavelot's attention where his wife's words had not. His wife then placed a plate of bread next to the bowl and stood waiting with her hands beneath her chin, palms together.

Father Stavelot said something in what I assumed was meant to be Latin, but the only word I understood was *Dominus,* which he pronounced *Domitianus,* the name of a Roman emperor whose name I've come across in ancient texts. Nevertheless, when he had finished speaking in his unknown tongue, I made the sign of the cross and considered the meal blest.

At last we each took our bread and dipped it into the bowl of stew. The taste was all that I had anticipated, and it was not without difficulty that I avoided the sin of gluttony. The priest ate in silence, as did I for the most part, but Madam Stavelot kept up her chatter between mouthfuls.

"Stavelot will be a bishop soon. That's why he studies so much," she said.

I managed a "Mmm" and a congratulatory nod in Father Stavelot's direction while I chewed a particularly succulent morsel of mutton. The priest responded with a smile that seemed to be more to himself than to acknowledge my gesture.

"He'll put me aside then, of course," madam said. "The pope favors celibacy in his bishops." She spoke in a matter-of-fact tone that brought no response from her husband. "It's best a woman not marry at all, I say. We should all take the veil and see how that suits them. Celibacy indeed! With no one to lie with when they wished, because we'd all be in a cloister, they'd be lusting and suffering. I'm certain of that, for I know the ways of men. At least in an abbey we'd have a roof over our heads and a chance to learn a thing or two. You made the right choice, Sister, I say."

"Don't vent your wrath at me, wife."

For a moment I stopped chewing, surprised that Father Stavelot had spoken at all.

"It is not my fault that you were made the devil's gateway, the unsealer of the forbidden tree," he said.

"And suppose you that it is my fault?" Madam's response came so quickly, I thought their argument must have been well practiced.

"Fault, you ask?" the priest said. "Because woman took the fruit and ate it, sin and death came into the world. Because of woman, even the Son of God had to die."

Madam was silent after that. I wasn't certain at first whether her silence was because of repentance for what our gender had done or because of anger she found hard to quell.

In a short time, Father Stavelot pushed himself away from the table and stood. "I will rest now," he said. "See that you make no noise." He disappeared behind a drape that was hung from a rod. I managed to see that the curtain was hung to conceal a bed.

As soon as he was out of sight, Madam took up her argument again while she poured the leftover stew back into the cooking pot and set about banking the fire.

"Adam didn't have to eat it just because it was offered, I say. Could he not have said no? Ah, well, who am I to question what the church fathers say? I suppose it's true that women are inferior to men. The learned ones claim that woman is born woman and not man because of a defect in our mother's womb. I suppose that's true as well. Why else would we be defined by our connection to man? Are we not called either virgin, prostitute, or wife?"

"I've never thought of that," I said as I wiped the bread crumbs from the table for her. To think of it now somehow troubled me, although I didn't tell her that. Of course, I had also heard and accepted the fact that woman is inferior, just as I accepted the fact that a girl child resulted from a defect while the babe grows in the womb. Madam's tone when she spoke of it made me think that in spite of her claim to the contrary, she did not truly accept those theories. I was troubled even more because now doubts and questions about the facts sprouted in my mind as well.

"You may never have thought of it, but it's true, Sister. A woman is defined by what she is to a man. To take the veil and remain a virgin makes her free, some say, but for all my claims that it is best to remain undefiled, I would not have missed bearing children. Those who survived are grown now, with children of their own, so the happy time of suckling a babe at my breast is gone as well. But 'tis more than the babes I would miss. I will miss the coupling with my man. Oh, I know a woman should never say such words, but God made the coupling to be enjoyed, I say. Why else would he have made it such a pleasure?"

She asked the question not rhetorically, but as if she expected an answer. All I could do was stammer.

"I . . . I'm sure I don't know. . . ."

"Ah, well, if my husband is to be a bishop, and I am to be put aside, at least I can say I have had a taste of carnal pleasures, and if I am honest, I pity those of you who have not. The future bishop was not always so sour and distracted, you know. Condemn me as sinner for saying this if you must, but I can be thankful that although the juices of passion still flow in my body, I am already three years past thirty and can expect to leave this world soon."

Speech failed me. I had never heard a woman—or anyone—speak in such a manner. She pitied me for never having tasted carnal pleasure? The church fathers, as well as the nuns at Münster-Bilzen, teach us that we are to be grateful not to be subjected to such debasement, and, as virgins, we are freed from our own bodies, which, by natural law, are subservient to a man. I felt enormously confused, especially since I had endured a measure of torture attempting to deny certain cravings that I thought to be sinful.

I was grateful when the kitchen chores were done and I could sleep, and I accepted madam's offer to share the bed with her and her husband. However, in spite of the weariness that overcame me because of the rigors of the journey, all the thoughts Madam Stavelot caused to tumble in my head made it difficult for me to fall asleep.

The next morning I was more than eager to resume my journey even though Madam Stavelot warned me that a storm was coming. She said she was certain of it because she felt a particular aching in her knees. Nevertheless, I was eager to be on my way.

I left under a clear sky, but by noon a heavy, glistening shroud of snowflakes came quivering and gliding down on my head and shoulders. When the snow obscured the road, I stopped at a peasant's hovel and was granted a scant meal of watery soup as well as lodging in a storage shed for grain, which I shared with a congregation of mice.

The north wind, whose name was Aquilon, invaded my shelter that night. It screamed as it forced itself through cracks in the walls of the wooden shed, bringing with it a driving rain, which turned to ice as it fell. I was too cold to sleep, even though I was covered with my own cloak and Adolpha's as well. When I thought I would surely die, the peasant's wife came out in the storm to rescue me.

"It's a bad notion to keep a woman out in this weather. Especially a woman of the church. Who knows but what you might be called a saint one day." She pulled me along, both of us keeping our heads down against the driving wind.

"There's scarce room," she whispered as she opened the door to her small cottage. I could see her husband and at least three children sleeping on straw mattresses on one side of the room, while a cow, her calf, and a goat slept on the other. "I advise you to sleep next to the cow. She's a warm body. I can vouch for that."

I nodded and scraped away some of the soiled straw before I lay down next to the animal. I was so cold I felt as if my bones and sinews had frozen, but the cow was indeed a warm body, and I slept with her close to me.

The next morning, I stepped outside into a strange land with tree branches made of clear glass glistening in the sun. The cold, driving rain and wind that had tormented me in the night had done this. Before I continued my journey, the peasant wife, who told me her name was Hilda, gave me a bowl of porridge mixed with warm milk fresh from the cow. The cow, bless her, warmed me from the inside as well as the outside.

After breakfast, Hilda sent me off with a warning: "Not wise to be traveling alone," she said. "Besides the weather there are wolves and Vikings along the way. You must beware the Vikings especially. Evil men they are, with horns that grow from their heads and an appetite for human flesh. They come down from the north in their great ships crafted in the shape of serpents and dragons. They come to kill and pillage and to work their evil spells. I dare not think what they would do to a woman. Even a nun."

I had never heard of Vikings, and, though I shivered with fear at the woman's description, I secretly hoped to see one—from a distance, of course. Before I left, I took both her hands in mine and kissed them in gratitude for what she had done for me.

I walked for another full day, grateful that the road I followed was well traveled enough that I could at least find footprints on the frozen ground and know that I would not go astray. There were no Vikings along my route, although I saw wolves from a distance. I stopped that night at a hermit's cell. He fed me from his store of roots, nuts, and mushrooms he had collected for the winter, and sent me away with another warning about Vikings, as well as a prediction that I would fall ill before the end of my journey.

By afternoon it rained again, and the hermit's prophecy about illness came true. My stomach cramped, and a watery flux flowed from my bowels. By that I knew the hermit was no prophet. It was only that he knew his roots and mushrooms all too well and that my stomach was likely not accustomed to them as his must have been. The sickness forced me to stop frequently, and I grew weak. By nightfall I could hardly walk, but, by the grace of God, I saw a cluster of buildings in front of me, which I took to be a village.

All of nature whirled around me at such a dizzying speed I could hardly stand, and the village disappeared.

14

Temsche
Autumn 794

Amelia

I was in a dark tunnel. It didn't occur to me that it might be odd that I could see through the darkness that filled the dark tunnel. I was conscious only of the fact that he needed me. I called his name.

"Charles. Charles, I am with you now."

"Amelia?" He sounded uncertain.

"Yes, I am with you now," I said, trying to reassure him. He was wounded. Near death.

"Where? I can't see you."

I sensed him slipping away from me. "Breathe," I cried. "Breathe, my love. Breathe. . . ."

"Yes," came a voice I didn't recognize. "You must take a deep breath. You've been ill."

I opened my eyes and saw a face. I was confused, because the face didn't belong to the king. It was a young face. Dark eyes, a dark beard, pleasing to look upon. I had no idea why he was staring at me with such concern.

"Who are you?" I asked.

"I am called Josep." His accent was unmistakable.

"You are a Jew." I tried to sit up, tried to look around for Charles, but Josep pushed me back with a gentle force onto a down-soft mattress that I saw was held by the frame of a wooden bed.

"And you are a Frankish Christian. A nun, it seems." His smile made his face seem younger still, boyish even.

"Why are you here?" I asked, feeling even more disoriented.

"I might ask you the same thing." He turned away from me to pick up a small bowl. "And I might also warn you that you should be more careful of what you eat."

"Eat?" I said.

"It is not wise to eat mushrooms. Some of them are deadly." He had the bowl to my mouth and placed a hand behind my back to bring me upright so I could drink. I could hear muffled voices coming from behind a curtain.

"You are a physician?" I asked.

"No."

I jerked back from him, not willing to trust that I should drink the liquid in the bowl.

"It will do you no harm," he said, sensing my fear. "It's nothing more than the broth of a fowl."

"Why are you giving it to me?"

"Because you are ill, and this will give you the nourishment you need to heal."

I looked into his face for a moment. His dark eyes seemed to smile at me, but there was sadness in them, too, as well as in the shape of his mouth. I reached for the bowl and drank some of the contents. It had the taste of heaven, so I drank more, and then more, until finally I drained the bowl, and all the while the young man was telling me to slow down.

"Where am I?"

"You are in my home. In the village of Temsche."

"Temsche? Is it true? Am I at last in Temsche?" I could hardly contain my excitement. I mouthed a silent prayer of thanksgiving and made the sign of the cross.

"I am always confused when you Christians do that," Josep said, making an awkward and very inaccurate attempt at crossing himself. "I'm never certain if you are warding off the devil or giving thanks."

"I am giving thanks, of course. God has brought me here safely. I am also thankful that he sent you to save me. But where is . . . ?"

Before I could ask where Charles was, a strong, hearty laugh erupted from somewhere deep inside Josep. "I'm not the first Jew you Christians think was sent to save you, but please, don't crucify me."

At first I was shocked to hear a man speak in such an irreverent and blasphemous manner about the Son of God, but then I remembered he was a Jew and most likely didn't understand that he was blaspheming. Mother Landrada told me the day would come when all people, even Jews, would be baptized and joined to Christ. She also said that one must be careful around Jews because they could be dangerous. I couldn't remember how or in what way they would be dangerous, however.

"I will not crucify you." Hearing myself say those words made me laugh. It seemed ridiculous to me that I would ever have reason to utter such a phrase. My senses were becoming sharper, the image of Charles lingering, but growing fainter.

"Ah, yes, I see that the broth has given you strength," he said. "At least strength enough to feel merry."

That made me blush, and I ducked my head, not knowing how to reply to his remark. As it happened, I didn't have to, since, in the next breath, he was questioning me.

"Pray tell me why you feel it is so important to be in Temsche that you set out alone on what was obviously a treacherous journey." All the while he was mixing and stirring ingredients he'd placed in a pottery bowl similar to the one he'd used for the broth.

"I was not alone from the start. My companion died on the way. Our abbess was told it would be only a two-day journey for us. Obviously her information was wrong."

"I am sorry about your companion," Josep said. I knew he spoke the truth. I saw it in his eyes. "But why the journey?" he asked again.

"It is my pilgrimage," I said. "My abbess said coming

here and helping with the needs of the village would help me decide whether or not to take my final vows."

"And just what do you expect to do here?"

"I am told it is a poor village. I will do what I can. I'm told also there is no church here, no priest."

"You learned all this at your abbey, I suppose. Where is this abbey?"

"Münster-Bilzen."

"Ah, yes, only two days' journey from the palace at Aix-la-Chapelle. And how is Landrada?"

"You know Mother Landrada?"

"I know her well. I would venture that Landrada heard of the needs of Temsche from a traveler. Perhaps from a merchant like me."

"Not a merchant, a bishop."

"Ah, a bishop," he said. "I should have known. It's not surprising that he gave you wrong information about the distance."

"And why do you say that?"

He shrugged, then chuckled. "Perhaps it's because we merchants know the roads better. We travel them more than the clerics."

"Perhaps your commodity is more difficult to sell than salvation, so you must travel more."

Josep laughed. "A wit, are you? Well, I believe my commodity is in as much demand as salvation. I'm a salt merchant. And Landrada always welcomed me, albeit reluctantly. I believe she's a bit wary of Jews. Here, drink this," he said, handing me the bowl in which he'd been mixing I knew not what.

I pulled back from the bowl and refused to touch it. "That is not broth."

"No, it is not broth. The mixture is three herbs that will settle your stomach. As I said before, I am not a physician. I am a merchant, but I am what passes for a physician in Temsche. I learned the craft from my mother."

"Your mother?"

"She was a midwife and healer."

"Oh, I see," I said, taking the bowl with a little less reluctance.

"So you've decided to trust me?" There was a teasing lilt to his question.

"I've decided to trust your mother. Women are the best physicians. They are natural caretakers and healers."

He laughed again. "You are young to be so wise, Sister. . . ."

"I am called Amelia, and I am not yet a nun, so you need not address me as Sister."

"Well, Amelia of Münster-Bilzen, your abbess was correct. Temsche is indeed a poor village and in need of help, and there is no church. No synagogue either, but I daresay you can't help with that."

It took me a moment to realize he wasn't serious, but was making an attempt at a jest. I had never met a person of his temperament, and I must admit I was both curious and fascinated.

"There are not many Jews here?" I asked, knowing that if there were I would have a difficult time learning to adjust to very many people with wit such as his.

"There are four of us. There is Isaac, the vineyard keeper; and there is me; my wife, Judith; and our son, Nathan. Perhaps you will never have the misfortune of meeting the vineyard keeper. He is called Isaac the Disgruntled because his vineyards produce so poorly. He would tell you he once had a good vineyard near Frankfurt, and that he sold it to buy one at Temsche because he thought the grapes would grow well in soil along the river. But now his grapes wither and his vines die and his spirit turns to vinegar."

"Perhaps it is only that he fails to understand the vines."

"Understand the vines, you say? You speak as a pagan, as if the vines have souls and can speak."

I knew this time that he was again making a jest at my expense. I was learning to recognize it by a certain light that twinkled in his eyes.

"Have you not read in the Book of Judges of the Hebrew Bible how the prophet told of the trees speaking among themselves? Does that mean your prophets speak as pagans, too?"

"Ah, you are a scholar, I see, and one with some wit." He sounded excited, as if he had just made a great discovery.

"I am no scholar. Only a poor novice in the service of God."

"Spoken like a true Christian. Always so predictably self-effacing."

It seemed he had, in some indefinable way, insulted me. I could think of no worthy response, so I changed the subject. "Do the other farmers of Temsche have as much difficulty with their crops as Isaac does with his vineyard?" I asked.

"Yes, thus the reason the town is so poor," he answered.

"Then perhaps I truly can be of some help. I know a bit about farming. I once helped the king's steward improve his agricultural methods."

"The king's steward? Is that a boast? Could it be you're not so self-effacing after all? I am beginning to like you more and more."

"You're quite right," I said, once again ducking my head and feeling ashamed. "I was being boastful. I ask your forgiveness as I ask it of our Lord. But it *is* true," I added in spite of myself. "I believe I truly can help farmers improve their yield."

He smiled to himself and seemed about to say something, which I am certain would have been another jest at my expense, but I spoke again before he had the chance.

"Why did you choose to be a merchant in such a poor village? Couldn't a merchant prosper better in a city?"

"Without a doubt."

"Then why are you here?"

"Isaac."

"Isaac?"

"Yes, that disgruntled old man is my father. He's plagued with the ailments of age. He could never survive without a kinsman nearby."

I was taken aback. Mother Landrada said Jews were crafty and dangerous, yet here was one who worried about his father's welfare.

"I will leave you now," Josep said, gathering up the herbs and bowls. "You will sleep for a while, and when you awake, I think you'll find you feel much better."

I started to protest and to tell him that I needed to be up introducing myself to the village leaders so I could start my work as soon as possible, but my tongue felt too thick to speak, and a very pleasant sensation that my body was drifting overcame me. I leaned back on the bed, prepared to enjoy for only a moment that lovely incorporeal feeling, perhaps to see Charles again. Had I really called him "my love"? Was he surprised to hear me say such a thing? I felt his presence and was aware that he felt mine, aware that he was smiling and that I smiled at him in return.

When I awoke, there was no one with me, and I was once again disoriented. It took me a moment to remember where I was and why I was there and why Charles was not with me. I could see a thin ribbon of light seeping around the curtain and more light ribbons unraveling themselves in the cracks between the slatted window next to me. That was daylight, I saw. How long had I slept? All night? More than one night?

I was about to get out of bed when a young, pretty face

framed by ripples of dark hair peered at me from the edge of the curtain. Her mouth made a perfect little surprised O when she saw that I was sitting up in bed. She recovered quickly and walked toward me holding on her hip a young child with hair even darker and curlier than hers.

"Good morning, Amelia. If you feel well enough to eat, I'll bring you some porridge."

"Thank you," I said, "and I thank you for your offer of porridge, but I need not eat it in bed." When she saw that I was getting out of bed, she reached a hand for me to grasp. "You must be Judith," I said.

"Yes," she said, still holding my hand while she used the other to keep her son secured on her hip. "My husband has put you under my care while he minds our shop."

As I walked out of the corner where I'd slept so long, I saw that the house of Josep and Judith was well-appointed, leading me to believe that Josep had been an even more successful merchant before he made the sacrifice to help his father.

There was a large hearth in the center of the room, a long table with chairs, several chests that I thought might have held clothes or linens, and two beds, one smaller than the other.

"My father-in-law insists that he have his own bed," Judith said when she saw what caught my eye. "He has gone for the day as well, trying to squeeze one more drop of wine from his poor grapes. He was able to gather them before the freezing rain, but there were precious few to gather."

When she had filled a bowl with porridge, she sat across from me and leaned toward me with her chin in her hand and an eager expression on her face while I ate.

"You are very brave to travel so far alone. And you no older than I am. Tell me, what was the journey like?"

"It was . . . it was grueling," I said.

"Oh, yes, but interesting as well," she said.

The excitement in her voice made me smile. "Yes, interesting," I said.

"And dangerous?"

"Sometimes."

"Tell me. Tell me everything. Start from the beginning. The day you left."

She was so eager I found it impossible not to accommodate her, so I told her the entire story, including the sad death of my beloved friend Adolpha, all the way up to the point that the hermit gave me mushrooms that made me ill, and I somehow found Temsche. I was not certain whether I should tell her about seeing Charles during my journey, since the encounter seemed so real, but it was my uncertainty that ultimately made me decide against mentioning it.

Judith cried at the death of Adolpha and laughed at the audacity of Madam Stavelot and was alarmed by the hermit and his mushrooms. I realized that our conversation had been entirely about me, but when I asked her about her own life, she brushed it aside and asked me more questions, this time about my abbey. She was especially interested in the books I had read and begged me to tell her what I had learned from them. Her little son fell asleep nursing at her breast, and I was in the middle of explaining Vitruvius's theory of architecture when Josep entered with a shriveled little man whose height brought him only to Josep's shoulders, and whose weight might have been less than mine. His expression was as shriveled as his body, as if time had sucked all contentment and pleasure from his soul.

Josep, by contrast, wore a pleasant look, but one that seemed to hide a kind of cynicism.

"Who is this?" the old man asked.

"The woman I told you will be our guest for a while."

"One of those holy virgins? She'll be staying here in the house with us?" His expression left no doubt that he considered that distasteful.

"Yes, Father." By that I knew the little man was the one called Isaac.

Isaac scowled at me. "Don't these Christian women know a woman was made for childbearing? They make themselves useless when they vow to be virgins." He made a disgruntled growling sound as he turned to his son and added, "Don't tell these Christians they've found a quick way to make themselves extinct."

Judith leaned toward me and whispered, "Don't be offended. Isaac doesn't like anyone."

"Are you Isaac of the vineyards?" I asked, pretending to be brave.

"She's speaking to me?" Isaac said, turning once again to his son. "This woman is speaking to *me*? And how does she know about my vineyards? You've spoken of my affairs with this gentile?"

"She says she can help increase the yield," Josep said.

"And you were fool enough to believe her? Well, I'm not fool enough to waste my time." With that Isaac turned away and left the house.

15

Temsche
Autumn, Winter, and Spring 794-795

Amelia

I expected everyone to be as embarrassed as I was over Isaac's display. But Josep and Judith were ignoring Isaac and laughing together over something one or the other had said.

"I'm afraid I must go," I said finally.

Judith gave me a surprised look. "Go? Where will you go?"

"I must find a place to stay."

"Can't you stay here?" Judith asked.

"Don't let Isaac make you feel unwelcome," Josep said at the same time. "You will learn to ignore him just as we do."

Judith nodded eagerly, making me feel as if she was encouraging me to stay. And I truly did want to stay. Having

Judith to talk to made my loss of Adolpha easier to bear. Yet, I wasn't sure I should, since they were not baptized Christians.

"We won't try to turn you into a Jew if you promise not to make us Christians," Josep said, reading the truth in my silence. I noticed that he still had that cynically amused look in his eyes.

"Really, I . . . I'm not certain of . . . that is . . ."

I was remembering Mother Landrada teaching that the synagogue would be joined to Christ at the end of time. Perhaps that meant I should be spared the arduous necessity of trying to convince my hosts to be baptized, knowing that God, in his wisdom, would receive the Jews as he saw fit.

"I would be humbly grateful to you if you would permit me to stay," I said.

Judith hurried toward me and kissed the side of my face. "That would be wonderful!"

Her enthusiasm made me laugh with joy as I hugged her.

"Perhaps you'd like to meet some of your fellow Christians," Josep said. "Come along. I'll introduce you to Conwoin first."

Within a few minutes, I was wrapped in my cloak and walking with Josep along a muddy road lined with the wood-and-mud-brick huts that made up the hamlet of Temsche. One of the buildings appeared to be a tavern, and there was a blacksmith and a carpenter and even a weaver.

Josep noticed where my gaze wandered. "Temsche is a

village of free peasants who own their own land," he said, "but most of them, like my father, have suffered too many poor harvests recently. My own family would starve if not for my willingness to travel with my salt." He paused and pointed to a hut in front of us. "That is Conwoin's house," he said. "A peasant farmer himself and the village elder."

We stood in front of the door to the little house, and Josep shouted our arrival. "Conwoin! Open your door. I have brought you the answer to your prayers."

"What does a Jew know about a Christian's prayers?" a voice shouted from inside. When the door opened, a ruddy-faced, blond giant of a man stood smiling down at us. His smile turned to a look of surprise when he saw me. "By all the gods and spirits, you've brought me a nun!"

"Not just any nun, Conwoin," Josep said. "This one says she can make your crops grow and increase your harvest and build you a church as well."

Conwoin seemed unable to speak for a few seconds. "A church?" he said finally. "What does a woman know of building churches? And farming?" He laughed, as if it were all a jest. When he sobered, he scrutinized me carefully. "Where does a Jew find a nun?" he asked, frowning.

"I'll tell you when you invite us in," Josep said.

"Of course! Forgive me. Come in. Warm yourselves by the fire." Conwoin stepped aside to allow us to enter.

A woman, whom I presumed was Conwoin's wife, sat in the corner spinning, while two small boys played at her feet. She was tall, with a sturdy, big-boned body and golden hair she wore in a braid. She gave me a curious stare but didn't speak. Her spinning wheel spoke for her, whirring out a message that said she was too busy to stop for small talk. She divided her attention between her skein of thread and the boys. Conwoin continued to stare at me.

"What know you of building churches?" His question sounded like a challenge.

"I have studied the architecture of Vitruvius." I kept my voice as steady and confident as possible.

Conwoin frowned. "You've studied . . . What did she say, Josep?"

"She said she can help you build a church."

Conwoin shook his head as he continued to stare at me. "I never saw a woman who could—"

The spinning wheel stopped suddenly. "You haven't seen a lot of things, husband," the woman said. "Hear her out." She spoke with an accent I didn't recognize.

A troubled look played across Conwoin's face as he appeared to be contemplating his wife's order. "All right, speak, woman," he said, addressing me.

I explained to him how I would establish a stone foundation and build upon it. In the sooty black dust near the hearth, I drew a diagram with my finger, of walls and pillars built to bear weight, and showed him where doors and windows could be placed. He watched, giving me careful attention, and his wife, whose name, I learned, was Brunheld, drew near to watch as well while she held one of the little boys on her hip. They both asked questions—Would there be room for a crucifix behind the altar? Should the doors swing in or out? Would there be a place for a basin of the holy water there? Or should it be placed here?

Josep, to my amazement, was as interested as Conwoin and his wife and even made suggestions that were so astute I knew he must have read Vitruvius, too.

"If you can do this, little nun, you will have saved our lives, if not our souls," Conwoin said. "The king threatens death if we're not baptized or if we don't attend Mass regularly—Jews excepted, of course," he added, turning to Josep. "But," he said, turning back to me, "he leaves it up to us to find a way to do it."

"The king holds his authority by the grace of God," I said, "and the guidance of the people of the kingdom to salvation is his primary mission. He holds you to no higher standard than he does himself."

I was surprised to hear myself defending Charles so vigorously. Furthermore, I was embarrassed, because I knew I sounded pompous. It was especially obvious when an uneasy silence fell upon us.

"God has sent us a way," Brunheld said, shattering the awful quiet.

"Perhaps he has, or perhaps he hasn't. We shall know soon enough," Conwoin said.

"And now let us talk of farming," Josep said, so quickly I suspected his motive was to avoid another uncomfortable silence. "She claims to have taught her farming secrets even to the king's steward," he added.

"The king's steward, you say?" Conwoin laughed. "A woman couldn't do that."

"You would do well to listen to this woman," Brunheld said.

Conwoin was once again chastened and listened along with Brunheld as I explained what I had learned about preparing the soil with marl and fertilizer as well as pruning and grafting the vines and fruit trees.

"The king's steward, you say?" Conwoin said again when I finished my explanation. He sounded as if he still wasn't convinced that I knew of what I spoke. He stood and paced back and forth with his chin in his hand for a moment. "I'll gather some men," he said at length. "You will tell them what you have told me. If we all agree that it's wise to try your methods, then we will try."

"I can't see how her methods could make the yield less than in recent years," Josep said.

Conwoin cast an alarmed look at him. "Never say things could not be worse or they will be." He crossed himself, exhibiting in that moment a mixture of his pagan superstition and the one true faith.

"And what of the church?" Brunheld said.

"We can start now and work until the winter stops us," Conwoin said. "Then, if it appears the woman is as wise as she claims to be, we will resume in spring, and you shall have your church." With that, he walked to the door and opened it—a clear signal that we were to leave.

We did indeed begin preliminary work on the church

immediately, digging and preparing a foundation until winter locked the ground in its frozen prison. Then I held informal sessions to teach the farming methods I had learned. Only a few came to sit at Josep's table and listen to me at first, but gradually more and more came. Isaac still refused to speak to me, but I did catch him listening once or twice, although he pretended not to.

Winter arrived in earnest, bringing wind that coughed and screamed and spit snow until the village and countryside were covered with white. Sometimes it left its long daggers hanging from the eaves of houses. Then I turned to helping Judith with her spinning and weaving and her constant stirring of the pot to keep us all fed. I cherished those moments when the two of us worked together. I would like to say that we always talked of heavy matters—God and death and salvation and faith. But it was not always so. Mostly we talked of life—mundane, important things that men find tiring. Often we laughed at wonderful things that were so light and effervescent and ordinary I no longer remember them.

"It's not so quiet as it once was, is it, Josep?" Isaac would say.

Or, "The house holds one child and the noise of a dozen, Josep."

Or, "One cackling hen is tiresome, two can send a man to eternal rest."

Seldom did he refer to me in other than a disparaging and indirect way. Never did he address me directly.

"Would you ask the one who sits beside your wife to hand me the ladle for dipping porridge, Josep?"

Or, "Tell the nun the hour is late. She should cut her prayers short so we can all go to bed."

Only in that slight and annoying manner was I ever hindered in practicing my faith. I was curious about the daily prayers of their household, and when I asked Josep about them, he explained that he was reading from the Torah.

"It is the same as your Bible," he said. When he translated the words, I recognized them as familiar passages from the book known as Deuteronomy. *Hear, O Israel: the Lord our God, is one Lord, and thou shalt love the Lord thy God with all thy heart and with all thy soul and with all thy might. . . .*

The prayers, which followed the reading, also in the strange language of the Jews, were not offensive to me when translated by Josep. The long recitation was called the Shemoneh Esrei, and began: *Blessed are you, O Lord our God, God of our fathers, the God of Abraham, Isaac and Jacob, great, mighty, revered God most high who bestows loving kindness, creator of all, who recalls the good deeds of the fathers, and who brings a Redeemer to their children's children for his name's sake, in love, o savior and shield. Blessed are you, O Lord, the shield of Abraham.*

It was with that prayer of praise that I understood that our God truly is the same, and pondered more deeply Mother Landrada's words about her former pagan gods. The prayer was long and included not only praise and thanksgiving, but supplication for deliverance from sin. It seemed to me that the Christian prayer known to me as the Lord's Prayer was a shortened version of that very long Shemoneh Esrei.

It is the practice of the Jews for men and women to be separated for prayers, and I learned to comply. I also learned the ritual of taking three steps forward and three backward before the prayers. I knew not the meaning the Jews attached to that, but I perceived that I was honoring the Trinity—the Father, Son, and Holy Spirit. I also learned when to bend my knees and when to bow. It was Judith who told me the knees were to bend at the word *blessed*, and we were to bow at the word *You* when it referred to God. Eventually, I learned to recognize the Hebrew words. It was the same God I worshiped, I thought, no matter that the language was not Frankish.

I continued my own prayers, as I have said, including giving thanks and asking a blessing before a meal, but I learned to say the birkat ha-mazon with my Jewish family, which was grace *after* meals. It was my decision that we can never be too thankful nor praise God too much, so I felt comfortable with the birkat ha-mazon.

The Jews have another strange ritual of washing their hands before they eat, which, I admit, I sometimes forgot to do. Josep said it represented a ritual cleansing similar to baptism, but I found it unnecessary, since baptism does not have to be repeated, and I saw no practical need for so much washing.

Another of their practices was to kiss one's fingertips and touch the mezuzah on the doorpost when one left or returned to the house. The mezuzah bears the words found in the Book of Deuteronomy I mentioned earlier. That passage in the Bible includes a commandment that the Jews are to place the words at their doorposts. Josep had encased them in a wooden cask and put them where it was commanded. I refused to follow the ritual because it seemed to me it was giving reverence to an inanimate object, which is the same as worshiping idols.

Josep laughed. "And what is the difference, pray tell me, in kissing the mezuzah and praying to wooden representatives of your god or your saints?"

I was hard-pressed to answer him, yet I still felt I could not be wrong on this count. Of course, I had no objection to reciting the prayer that accompanied the ritualistic reverence to the mezuzah: *May God guard my going out and coming in now and forever.* What hint of idolatry could possibly be attached to that?

Isaac scowled at first when I joined in their rituals. He called it a sacrilege. Eventually, he learned to stop his grumbling, although I considered it no more than resignation on his part, certainly not approval.

Another habitual prayer was to thank God for the wine we drank. *Blessed are you, Lord our God, creator of the fruit of the vine.* Since the harvest had been poor for several years, even Isaac lacked enthusiasm when he recited that prayer. I could not blame him. The wine had a sharp taste and was full of dregs.

In spite of the long, cold winter, life was not dull. Visitors were frequent at the house, mostly because Josep was what passed for a physician in the village. He gave them herbs boiled in water for the cold-weather sickness and gallons upon gallons of the broth of fowl, particularly of chicken, which he said his mother told him would cure almost any sickness.

I was familiar with many of the herbs because I had gathered them myself in the forest near Münster-Bilzen, and I often helped Josep with his patients.

Conwoin's wife, Brunheld, came once, filled with fear, and would speak with no one but me.

"We have no priest!" Brunheld said in her odd accent. Tears streaked her gaunt face. "But you are a woman of the Church. You will know where I must go, where I must die. No Jew will know how to help me."

Josep, who never relished his role as physician, was not insulted. He was only too happy to turn Brunheld, or anyone else who would allow it, over to me.

Brunheld insisted that I speak with her alone behind the curtain that separated my sleeping quarters from the rest of the house. Once we were in the little room, she rolled up the sleeves of the robe she wore and showed me the patches of scaly, raw, and bleeding skin on the inside of her elbows.

"It's here as well," she said, weeping as she raised her long hair from the back of her neck to show me another spot of the eruptions. "It's leprosy," she whispered while I inspected the spots by the light of the candle I held. "I'll not get too close to Josep and his wife, and especially not the child, for fear I will pass it on to them. Leprosy is a curse, you know, an unclean curse that can contaminate any who come in contact. But God will keep you from it, because you have surrendered your life to Him." She began to cry again. "I shall have to be sent away, I know. But why has God punished me? I have done nothing wrong."

I put my candle on the table and held her hand while I rubbed the sore place on her arm to comfort her. "Have no fear," I said. "I've seen this before, and what you have will contaminate no one else."

"I will surely die." Sobs racked her body.

"In time we all will die, but your time is not today," I said. I kissed her arm, still trying to soothe her. I had seen the ailment on one of the nuns at Münster-Bilzen. She was a highly excitable and easily agitated woman whose skin eruptions worsened when she fell into one of her anxious and nervous states. Mother Landrada said her ailment was common among people of that temperament, and that the best medicine was to calm the person. She gave the nun an ointment made of pulverized herbs mixed with the rendered fat of a pig and soothed her with prayer and words of encouragement. I had none of the ointment and knew not where to get it, but I could offer soothing words.

"You have no leprosy on your body," I said. "Pray and seek peace and contentment in God the Father, Son, and Holy Spirit, and your disease will be cured." Then, as an afterthought, I removed the crucifix from the rope that is always tied at my waist and placed it on each of her arms and on the back of her neck.

She went away only partly consoled, but within a few days the rough and bloody spots on her skin healed. To my great embarrassment, she announced to the village that I miraculously healed her, and she began to call me a saint.

None of my protestations or my explanations that it was God who had healed her would do.

"God works through his saints," she insisted.

Others came to me for healing after that, which I could sometimes accomplish with the help of Josep and, of course, the help of God.

My reputation served only to make Isaac scowl at me more. It was a winter in which my patience was too often tried. To add to my misery, I could not stop thinking of the king, nor of his arms around me, nor of the strange visit I had made to him.

It concerned me that I could no longer effect that kind of visitation. Where was he now? Still fighting the Saxons? Not likely, I decided. Not in the dead of winter. He had most likely returned to one of his palaces. Or had he not returned at all? Had he died on the battlefield? He seemed to be so locked in darkness that death seemed a strong possibility. That thought frightened me and made me long for him more than ever. On too many nights my pillow was wet from the tears I shamefully shed for him.

Spring brought me some healing, and I knew I was not the only one in the house of Josep who rejoiced at the sight of melting snow and green shoots and the promise of freedom from so much close communion.

16

TEMSCHE

SPRING–SUMMER 795

Amelia

I kept my custom of rising early each morning to pray and follow the holy offices, and I was just finishing matins one spring morning before dawn when I heard singing voices. My first thought was that a chorus of angels had arrived to announce the return of Jesus from heaven. That thought was quickly discarded, though, when I realized the sound was more bawdy and raucous than angelic.

Hurrying to my window, I opened the shutters and saw a host of people—men, women, children—all singing as they walked up a small hill just outside the village. Several of them were carrying small baskets. I was still staring at them in wonder when I heard Judith calling me from behind the curtain that separated my bed from the main room. Her voice was soft and quiet, as if she were trying not to awaken anyone else.

"Amelia, are you awake?"

"Yes," I said and hurried to push back the curtain. "Is something wrong?"

"Wrong? Oh, of course not," Judith whispered. "I thought you might want to join the rest of the village for the celebration." She gave a quick glance over her shoulder. "Josep said you wouldn't approve, but you will go, won't you?"

"What sort of celebration?"

"In honor of Eostre." Judith was slightly breathless with excitement. "I thought she was a Christian saint, but Josep says she's a pagan goddess. I don't know how he keeps them straight." She waved her hand in dismissal. "No matter, it's such a merry celebration, I know you'll like it."

"I . . . I'm not certain that I . . ."

I knew, of course, that I should be very certain that I would not go. It would no doubt be a most egregious sin for me to join in a pagan ceremony, but Eostre was the goddess Mother Landrada had worshiped before she became Christian, the same goddess she claimed gave our Easter celebration its name. "Yes," I said, surrendering to a temptation too great to conquer. "Of course I'll go with you."

We left the house quietly, wrapped in our cloaks to protect against the cool spring morning, and hurried to join the rest of the villagers. We were the last ones up the hill. The raucous singing had stopped, and Conwoin was just beginning to speak. His back was turned to the crowd as he faced the red glow of the rising sun with his arms stretched out from his body, palms up, as if to greet the sun.

"We welcome you, O Eostre of the rising sun and the dawning of a new season. As the sun rises, you raise your head from your long winter sleep to smile upon us and to receive the seed of your consort to nurture in your holy womb until the time of Haligmonath, when you will become the Earth Mother and deliver unto us your issue."

He spoke in the old Saxon tongue used most often by peasants, but it was a language I knew well, since many of our community at Münster-Bilzen also spoke that language, and it was Mother Landrada's native tongue.

All around us, small round objects hung from branches of the budding trees. I knew without having to inspect them too closely that the round things were freshly baked buns given as offerings to the goddess. They would be decorated with a Christian cross made of sugar, or, if the pagan tradition still held, with the shape of a wheel with eight spokes to symbolize the cycles of the seasons.

"Holy Mary, Mother of God, we welcome you from your long sleep," Conwoin continued. "Bless us with your reawakening. Nurture our crops in the holy womb of the earth as you nurtured your son, Our Lord Jesus Christ, in your own womb."

His mixing of pagan incantations with Christian prayers was common among many people in the Frankish kingdom, but it was disconcerting to me, nevertheless.

"Don't be offended," Judith whispered. "They just want to make sure the prayer is heard by at least one god."

"There is only one God, and you know it as well as I."

I was shocked at her statement, but her pretty face was so flushed with happy excitement, I couldn't be angry with her.

Just as Conwoin completed his ritual and turned around to face the crowd, the entire group erupted into shouts and laughter and general chaos. I could make no sense of what they were doing until I saw them taking eggs from the baskets they held and rolling the eggs down the hill. Conwoin, with his arms still raised, was saying something I couldn't make out clearly, except that he was speaking of the rolling and turning of the sun and the seasons. The people followed the eggs down the hill, shouting and laughing.

"Come along," Judith said, taking my hand. "If we're lucky we can get some of the eggs and some of those hot cross buns. They say if you eat them, you'll have good luck all year."

I was reluctant to join in the pagan ritual, but her excitement was infectious, and I found myself laughing and running down the slope with her. Once we were at the bottom of the hill, we picked up as many of the eggs as we could hold in the folds of our skirts.

"We'll go to Conwoin's house," Judith said, her face ruddy and shining with excitement. "Brunheld bakes the best hot cross buns of anyone." She ran ahead of me, and I stopped, holding the eggs in the fold of my skirt, watching others running and laughing, and suddenly aware of what I was doing. I was a representative of the holy Christian church, an applicant to become a bride of Christ, participating in a pagan ritual. I let go of the fold in my skirt, allowing the eggs, pagan symbols of fertility, to drop to the ground and shatter.

When I arrived back at the house of Josep, there was no one there except Isaac, who sat scowling as he watched the merriment from an unshuttered window. I was weeping silently as I walked past him to the small area behind the curtain that had been granted me. I wept not only because of the pagan revelry going on outside, but, if I were to be honest, because I could not join them. I could only be another Isaac who watched and scowled.

The revelry lasted for only one day. It was too soon to plant the fields because the nights still brought frost, so we spent our time working on the church. Within a few days we had at least a shell of a building. Each Sunday I made sure the villagers assembled there. Although I could not say Mass or serve Holy Communion, I could at least read from holy scriptures and teach the people to recite prayers. I could also caution them against their pagan rituals and beliefs. The services were well attended, for which I was grateful and gave thanks to God that I might be making a difference among the pagans, since none of them, not even Conwoin, argued against giving up their heathen ways.

My pride in my holy accomplishments was shattered within weeks. On the day the villagers called Wealburges, a long pole was erected in the center of the village with streamers flowing from the top. Young men and women held the ends of the streamers and danced around the pole, weaving the streamers in an intricate pattern. Once the weaving was done, the young people stole away to the woods for coupling. When they were gone, older people performed the same dance and ran into the woods for the same reason. I knew about all of this from Mother Landrada's stories. The winding dance around a pole that represented a body part peculiar to men was believed to grant fertility to the dancers as well as the fields. It was one of the ceremonies the Church forbade, since the coupling was not always between married partners. Once again I retreated to my corner to pray for the people and that they would leave their pagan ways.

That night I dreamed of Charles. Only it was more than a dream. He came to me in the same way I had gone to him before, when I knew he was wounded. We danced together, winding around our own maypole until we slipped away into the forest.

The morning after Wealburges Day, the farmers all seemed to be in peculiarly good moods as they assembled in the fields to begin planting. I felt refreshed myself, as if my dream had given me rebirth. I was as eager to begin as the others were and was busy for weeks, going from one field to the next, demonstrating the techniques I had taught during the winter. I spent many hours pushing a plow and showing the men how to drop seed in the furrows made by the plow, rather than strewing them in broad casts across the fields. By night my shoulders and arms ached, and I fell asleep more than once before my prayers were all said, but never without thinking of the king and praying for his well-being. I was grateful to be too tired to long for him or to meet him in my dreams in that physical way that was so strange and frightening to me.

I thought it best that I discipline myself now not to have such encounters again. I also spent a great deal of time teaching the people that the practices of Wealburges Day were sinful. They all listened patiently like good children, but I had no sense that they were inclined to heed my warning.

"It will be a good year," Conwoin said to me one day after a Sunday service I conducted. "The earth has already sent up green shoots, and it is not even time for the equinox. Our prayers to the Holy Mother of God have been heard." He made the sign of the cross as he spoke, giving me confidence that he was referring to the Virgin and had forsaken his pagan goddess.

It was not until a day or two later, when I found a clay figure of a woman with large hips and prominent breasts placed in a position to watch over Conwoin's field, that I knew my confidence was ill-placed. I had only to walk a short distance to another man's field to find a replica of the statue also set strategically to watch over the crops. I had seen the figure before in peasant fields near Münster-Bilzen. It was the goddess Eostre, this time without the ears of a hare.

Rage, along with a fear I didn't understand, replaced the blood in my veins, and an animal-like cry erupted from my throat as I grabbed the statue and ran to Conwoin's house in the village.

"Conwoin! Conwoin, let me in," I cried as I pounded the door to his house with my fist.

It was Brunheld who opened the door. "What's wrong? What has befallen us?" Her face was drained of blood, and her eyes were frightened. Conwoin was hurrying toward us from the opposite end of the room.

"This," I said, pushing past Brunheld and holding the vile statue in front of me. "This is what is wrong! This is the evil that has befallen us."

Conwoin looked at me, puzzled. "Eostre? The Earth Mother?"

"How many times have I told you these gods are evil?" My hands were shaking so that I could hardly hold the statue, and tears of anger filled my eyes. "How many times do I have to show you the way, tell you about the one true God? Why do you resist me? Why do you turn away from salvation?"

"Evil?" Brunheld looked as puzzled as Conwoin as she looked first at me and then at him.

"Eostre is . . . is like the Holy Mother of God," Conwoin said, fumbling for words. "She . . . is the mother of all of us. See her breasts? Her wide hips made for holding up her womb? Don't you see her in the eyes of Mary? They . . . they are the same. . . ."

"No!" I screamed. "They are not the same. How dare you compare the Mother of God to this!" I threw the statue to the hard stone floor and watched it shatter into a rain of clay and dust.

Brunheld sucked in her breath in alarm and dropped to the floor, crying as she scooped up the pieces into her hands.

Conwoin could only stare at me while a black sea of horror swelled in his eyes. "Must you destroy our gods to save yours? What kind of god despises his own kind? Out! Get yourself out of my house."

I ran with as much speed as I could manage to the shell of a church and fell on my knees, unable to utter even the meanest of prayers because of my sobs.

Neither Conwoin nor Brunheld came to prayer services with the rest of us after that. In time, some of the others who had heard of my destructive act stayed away as well. Yet almost everyone, including Conwoin, came to work on the church throughout the spring and summer, when work in the fields slowed. Working alongside Conwoin and the others who resented my act was, of course, awkward and uncomfortable. Conwoin would not speak to me and even made an effort not to work alongside me.

I was saddened by all of that and tried to approach him once as he was building a frame for one of the windows.

"It distresses me that you avoid me and that you refuse to worship with the rest of us," I said.

He glanced up at me briefly without stopping what he was doing, but he said nothing.

"I only want you to understand that it was a false god I destroyed. It is for your own benefit that you turn away from false gods, lest you burn in hell. Can you not see that it is because I care about you that I . . ."

He picked up his tools and walked away from me before I could explain to him that his very life as well as his soul could be in danger. Both God and the law of the land forbade the worship of pagan gods. As I watched him retreat, I felt myself swallowed by the gaping mouth of despair.

I worked harder and longer hours on the church, hoping to rescue myself from the darkness that surrounded me. Even in my sorrow, I couldn't stop thinking of Charles. If he was alive, would he go looking for me at the abbey? If he did and learned I'd left, would he come for me? I pushed that thought away with shame. That was not something I should be anticipating. And anyway, he'd had plenty of time to find me by now, if he'd wanted. He'd forgotten me, of course, and I would forget him as well.

"You spend yourself building the church," Judith said. "See how thin you are? You seldom take time to eat or rest. It damages your spirit, friend. I never see you smile or hear you laugh."

I hardly bothered to respond to her except to mumble that the work was important.

"Some of the people are angry with you." A worried frown marred her pleasant face when she said that. "I hear them say you destroyed their god."

A response erupted from my soul immediately, since that was the root of my unhappiness.

"Of course I destroyed the god. It was a false god. A graven image. Your own religion forbids such things."

Still frowning, Judith looked at me for several seconds

before she spoke. "Perhaps it's only that their eyes see things differently. Perhaps they see the true god somewhere within the graven image."

Her words shocked me. "Do my ears deceive me, Judith? Have you forsaken the God we hold in common for the golden calf?"

Judith's eyes flashed. "Don't pronounce judgment against me, Amelia. The path you walk to find God seems as pagan a ritual to me as setting an image of Eostre in the fields does to you."

"Do you dare call the God I worship pagan?" My voice rose in a blast of anger.

"Perhaps, but I would never call him false." Her voice, in contrast to mine, was quiet. For a reason I could not understand, that quiet voice infuriated me.

The next morning, I left the house at dawn, as soon as I prayed the office of matins and before anyone else was awake. I worked furiously, stopping only for water or when I had to relieve myself, as if my labor would somehow vindicate me. I was angry with Judith because she had been unfair. I had been tolerant of her family's faith, believing the truth would eventually be revealed to them. But she repaid my tolerance and faithfulness with sympathy for the pagans and, so far, no inclination that she was going to accept Christ. Instead, she even called him a pagan god.

To help me learn patience and to strengthen myself against the blasphemy that was all around me, as well as to keep Charles out of my thoughts, I worked still harder in the fields and on the church. I was so intent and consumed by the work of pounding iron nails into the hard wood of a door frame that I was unaware of anything happening around me. I didn't see the little girl who toddled up to the structure to watch her father cut planks of wood from the immense tree trunk. I didn't hear the creaking and groaning sound behind me, and I was only dimly aware of the shouts just before the doomsday sound of destruction filled my ears and I saw the south wall of the church fall outward, toward the child, knocking her down.

Next came a commotion of dust, falling debris, shouts—all of it caught in a tangled web of confusion. It seemed to take an inordinate length of time for me to reach the child, and by the time I was at her side, her father was holding the limp body with its tiny arms dangling, eyes open and staring at nothing, mouth agape. Somehow the mother appeared and snatched the girl from the father, and I heard her screaming, "She's dead! She's dead!"

Something happened to me in that moment, something that I find difficult to describe, except to say that I was suddenly, almost painfully, filled with a mixture of power and . . . what? Fear? Rage? I shall never know. I pulled the child from her mother's arms. At the same time I heard a loud voice crying out, "No! Nooooo! Don't die! Live! Live!"

I knew it was my own voice when I saw the little girl blink her eyes, focus them on me. Then, not recognizing me, she cried, "Mama! Mama!"

Her mother took her from my arms and, holding her

to her chest, spoke to her with soft, soothing words as she walked away from the crowd, oblivious to everything except the living, breathing child in her arms.

For a brief moment I was afraid the crowd would claim I'd performed another miracle, since I happened to be the one holding the child when she revived. That did not happen, but what followed surprised me even more.

"Conwoin told us our luck would change after she destroyed the image!" a man shouted. "This is a warning. Next time someone will surely die."

I heard a buzzing all around me. I recognized it as the sound of fear. I could distinguish only a few words. "Eostre is angry." "Bad luck . . ." "Amelia has cursed us." "Someone will die." I felt a blow strike my back. I staggered and almost fell. Then there was another and another as I tried to move away.

"It was an accident. Nothing more!" I cried. I tried to speak again, but my voice was swallowed by the angry noise of the crowd. It was all I could do to push through the mass of bodies and find my way to the house of Josep and Judith.

As soon as I opened the door Judith ran to me, alarmed. "What happened? We heard the noise and the shouting, and Josep ran to see . . . You're crying! You've been hurt!"

"No," I said, wiping the tears from my face. "My body has not been harmed. They blame me for . . ." I saw Isaac emerging from the corner where he kept his bed. He was staring at me with curiosity, but he spoke not a word. "They blame me for the wall of the church falling down," I said, trying to ignore him. "A child was hurt when it fell, and the people say it was because their goddess was angry that I destroyed her image."

Judith said not a word, but I thought I saw blame in her eyes, too.

I made an attempt to defend my actions. "They worship false gods. I was only trying to . . . Oh, Judith, what have I done?"

She encircled me in her arms, trying to comfort me. "You have done what you thought you should do," she said.

"But I'm not at all sure it is what I should have done." I was sobbing as I clung to her. My sobs woke little Nathan, and Judith had to go to him. I went to my own bed and did my best to pray. I stayed there until Judith pushed the curtain back to tell me to come eat supper.

At first I thought of declining, but I didn't want to appear sullen and pouting, so I followed Judith. Josep and Isaac sat near the hearth conferring in hushed voices. They both looked up as Judith and I emerged.

"That was an ugly scene in the village today," Josep said to me.

"You saw it?" I asked.

"I stepped outdoors when I heard the noise. When I heard the crashing sound, I thought someone might be hurt, and I might be needed."

"Someone *was* hurt." I found it difficult to look at him.

"I know. The child of the farmer Rupert. When I heard

of it, I went to offer my services. Her bones are supple and none were broken, but she suffered a blow to her head that robbed her of consciousness for a short time. I've seen such things before. She will live."

I nodded, too sickened by the memory to speak.

"Some say you healed her."

My eyes widened when Josep said that.

"But others give you no such credit and say you caused her harm when you—"

"We know, Josep," Judith said. "She told us what they say."

Josep acknowledged Judith with a nod of his head and spoke no more, but he kept his gaze trained on me for several seconds, giving me the feeling that he, too, blamed me.

"I wanted to stop them from worshiping false gods, but I fear I've gone about it wrong," I said. "I should have . . . should have been . . . Oh, I don't know how I could have done it. I believe I made the wrong decision to come here in the first place. This may be God's way of telling me I'm not fit to be a nun."

"Now is not the time to decide that. Not when you're distraught," Josep said.

"Will you talk all night? It's time to eat," Isaac said. He was already at the table.

When the rest of us joined him, the mood was somber. It was as if my sadness had affected all of them. At least the others were able to eat, but I found it impossible to put even one morsel in my mouth. I realized my mood had further poisoned Isaac's ill humor when he left the table early, while there was still food in the pot. He went to the corner where he kept his bed and rummaged in the chest next to it. A few minutes later he left the house carrying a bundle in his arms. He still had not returned when the rest of us retired to our beds.

"Is he all right?" I heard Judith ask Josep after we had all gone to bed.

"Yes," Josep said. "He is in no danger."

"But it's late," Judith said.

"He has no woman to warm his bed, so it matters not that the hour is late. His only pleasure is his . . ."

I heard no more after that as their voices became whispers. Though I slept little, I never heard Isaac return to the house that night. When I emerged to help Judith prepare breakfast, he was already gone to his vineyard, probably to escape my dark mood.

17

TEMSCHE
SUMMER–AUTUMN 795

Amelia

We heard shouts coming from the village before the morning porridge was hot.

Judith looked frightened. "Josep!" she called, when it became clear some of the people were shouting my name. They seemed to be getting closer to the house.

Josep was seated at the table with a reed stylus and a wax tablet, calculating what I supposed were inventories of salt. He glanced up when Judith called, and in the next second jumped up from his chair and ran to the door. By this time someone was banging his fist on it while voices shouted.

"Come see! Come see the church! See what Amelia has done!"

My heart came to my throat.

"Stay where you are," Josep said, going to the door. "I'll talk to them."

"No," I said, walking toward him. "They've come for me. I want no harm to come to anyone else."

Josep tried to hold me back, but I jerked away from him and opened the door. "If you've come for me, I'll go peacefully," I said, "but no harm must come to . . ."

To my great surprise the man who had knocked at the door fell at my feet and kissed the hem of my robe. "God has blessed us with a saint. We beg your forgiveness."

"A saint? Why do you—"

"You've given us miracles!" someone shouted from the street.

"I don't understand. What . . . ?"

"The church," someone else shouted. "It's a miracle!"

I saw Isaac trying to force his way through the crowd to get into the house, but I lost sight of him as someone took my arm and pulled me into the street. It was a gentle pull this time, and there were no harsh blows to my body. In the next moment I saw the miracle they proclaimed.

There were once again four walls of the church standing. The shattered one had been miraculously restored overnight.

"We doubted you at first," one of the men said. I recognized him as the father of the child who was injured when the wall fell. "You healed my daughter and you restored the church. Your power is greater even than that of the goddess."

"No, you are mistaken. I didn't . . ." I was unable to finish my sentence, and no matter how much I continued to deny the credit, it was impossible for me to make anyone understand.

"Leave her be," someone shouted. "Can't you see how you've frightened her? Get back to your work and enjoy her miracles." I recognized the voice. It was Conwoin coming to my rescue.

Finally the others left, a few at a time, until only Conwoin and I stood facing each other inside the four walls of the church.

"You are a woman of great power and great compassion as well," he said. "I will never forget what you have done."

"But I didn't—"

"This was your greatest kindness," he said, pointing to something in the corner where the restored wall met the wall at the front of the church.

I turned to look and saw before me a clay statue of the goddess Eostre looking back at me in her usual posture, with her hands holding up her breasts and a faint smile on her face.

"She is the same as the Christian goddess. She is our lady. Like the Christian goddess who gave birth, she is our lady of the nativity. Our goddess gives birth to the new season. I thank you for understanding that."

"I . . . I didn't—"

"I know you acted in haste when you broke the goddess. We acted in haste as well when we condemned you. But no harm has been done. Thanks be to God," he added in what seemed to be an afterthought.

I had no idea what god he meant to thank, but he gave me no chance to question him or even to deny again any responsibility for the miracle. He left, hurrying home for his morning porridge before we began work on the church again. I was left alone to stare at the wall and feel the awe of having witnessed a miracle. I reached out my hand to touch the structure, to make certain it was really there. My fingertips barely touched the sturdy wood when I heard a voice behind me.

"It took him all night, you know."

It was Josep's voice, and I turned around in surprise to face him.

"Took him all night?" I was puzzled.

"Isaac. He worked all night. By torchlight."

"Isaac?"

"I knew what he was doing when I saw him leave with that bundle he always uses to carry his tools."

"Isaac," I whispered, unable to fully comprehend. "But why would he . . . ?"

"He didn't tell me why. Maybe it was because he saw how distraught you were."

I shook my head. "But he doesn't like me. He won't even speak to me. Why would he do this?"

Josep laughed. "I told you he's a disagreeable old man. Who knows why he did it? Maybe to thank you for teaching him to grow more and better grapes. Maybe he just didn't like the somber mood you brought to our table."

"But to do this! He's not even Christian." I found it impossible to express my amazement.

"He is cantankerous, but he's not without sympathy," Josep said.

I turned to leave the church. "I must hurry to tell the others. They think I performed a miracle."

"Wait!" Josep grabbed my arm to stop me. "You don't want to make him angry. Let him tell them if he wishes them to know."

"But . . ."

"You don't want to make him angry," he said again, but with more emphasis this time.

We stared at each other for a few moments, I with impatience, and Josep with what appeared to be desperation, before we both gave in to laughter.

That night as we ate our supper, I mentioned the church wall.

"The villagers say I have caused a miracle by restoring the wall." I dipped my bread into the communal pot of vegetables and barley and continued without looking at Isaac. "They are being foolish, of course. It was no more my doing that the wall was raised overnight than it was my fault it fell. I say there's another miracle maker among us."

There was a long silence before Isaac turned to Josep. "There's much talk in the village of that wall in the pagans' temple. Have you heard it?" He was acting as if I hadn't mentioned it at all.

"I have heard the talk," Josep said.

"They talk of miracles because it was restored." Isaac laughed, a wicked little sound. "The miracle is that it stood at all the first time. The fool who planned the structure did not build well on the foundation. Why, the wall was hardly attached to the foundation at all. It required upright posts rising from the foundation to fasten the wall to. Foolish, I say."

"Perhaps a lesson was learned by that," Josep said. "Whoever restored it knew how to use the foundation, it seems."

Isaac's only reply was an indignant snort and a glance at me.

There are days in the summer, and blessed days they are, when the farmer must leave the fields and allow crops to do the work themselves. Plants grow and mature and put on their fruit, and the farmer says that his crop is "laid by" until weeding or watering or harvesting needs to be done. It was during those laid-by times that we worked harder on the church and finished it just before the harvest month.

It was also on one of those summer days that a stranger came to the village looking for me. Conwoin brought him inside the church, where I was bent over, helping construct the altar.

"Amelia," he called. "This messenger seeks you."

I stood and winced as I felt a muscle in my back contract too quickly. The stranger, who held a folded vellum in his hand, approached me.

"You are Amelia of Münster-Bilzen Abbey?" He spoke in a dialect of the Germanic tongue.

"I am."

"This is for you," he said, thrusting the vellum at me.

It was rare for anyone to receive a written message, particularly rare for a humble novice such as I. Because of that, I was hesitant to accept it, fearing that it bore bad news. Perhaps news of the death of Mother Landrada. I waved a hand at Conwoin, signaling him to leave. He was reluctant to turn away from so important an occasion, but I wanted to be alone if it was bad news I had to read. I was still reluctant to accept the parchment, however.

"It's best you take it," the man said, still thrusting it at me. "It's from the king."

I felt my breath catch in my throat. Charles was dead! Someone in the court—Einhard, perhaps—had sent me a message. My hand shook as I reached for the vellum.

The man gave me a suspicious look, as if he might have thought I'd been summoned by the king because of some crime I'd committed.

"I took it from the hands of a man now dead," he said as I unfolded the letter. "Near frozen to death when I found him, but he lived long enough to tell me the message was meant for you and where to find you. He said he'd learned where you were from an abbey called Münster-Bilzen."

"You say he was frozen to death?" I hardly recognized my own choked voice. "The message was sent in the winter? It's almost winter again."

The man shrugged. "Couldn't risk traveling in winter and dying myself just to bring it to you, could I? I got it to you as soon as I could, even though the king's messenger paid me not at all. I saw it as my duty to the king to take up his task."

I knew he was lying about not being paid. The fine boots he wore and the silver hilt of a soldier's sword that hung at his side told me the dying soldier had either given them to him or the man had taken them from the corpse.

There was no explanation forthcoming as to why he'd not brought the message to me during the spring or summer as the man stood before me, waiting. I thought at first that he was waiting for me to read the letter, until I realized he wanted me to pay him.

"I have nothing to give you except a blessing," I said.

"You have shoes," he said.

"What?"

"I have a wife who has no shoes. You have a fine pair upon your feet."

I looked down where the toes of the shoes peeked out from under the hem of my robe. They were shoes such as peasants might wear, with wooden soles, but sturdy. I took them off and gave them to him, knowing full well that even if he had a wife with no shoes, she might never see them. The man would very likely barter them for something for himself. I also knew full well that it is a sin to judge a man in such a way, but God has given me a mind to reason out the truth.

I clutched the letter to my breast for a few seconds before I had the courage to read it. The man stepped back a few paces and waited. I knew he waited to see if there was a reply, for which I would have to find a way to pay him again.

I almost cried when I saw the writing, with the letters on the parchment overly large and crudely shaped, such as a child might draw. How many times had I heard the king lament the fact that he could not write well? What courage it must have taken to attempt this! All of that made the letter, as well as its author, all the more precious to me.

The message was short and difficult to read:

I badle the Sasns til sno fals. You cm to me in dark. Whn am wel I cm to yo at abi to spek of

The rest of the message was blurred by dampness. There was not even his signature, yet I knew the words were his, and I was startled. He *had* seen me, and I had seen him. It was not a dream. But what did he mean by "Whn am wel"? Did he mean to say *well*? Was he still not well? And what did he wish to speak to me about? Was it more advice he wanted? Was he seeking my counsel on behalf of his daughter, who would need to be instructed about the abbey she would be granted? Or would he speak of love? I dared not even think of such a thing.

"Will there be a reply?" the man asked.

I hesitated, thinking of all the things I wanted to say

to Charles, thinking of how I wanted to tell him that I thought of him often and longed for his touch. That I, too, was aware of our strange meeting. But that was not something I should do.

"No," I said, finally. "There will be no reply."

"There is plenty of room to write your message on the back of the parchment," the man said, knowing I would not be likely to have writing materials of my own.

"There will be no reply," I said again.

He turned away, walking toward the village gate.

"Wait!" I called to his back, and when he turned to face me, I asked, "Have you news of the king? Did he fare the winter well? Does he do battle again? Or is he at home in one of his palaces?"

"I am not privy to the king's counsel, Sister. I know nothing of his battles or of his palaces." With that remark, which was spoken in a sullen voice, he turned away again.

I could not get Charles out of my mind after that, wrong as I knew it was for me to think of him in such a manner as I did. I unfolded the parchment and reread the message dozens of times. Sometimes I would simply look at the letters and imagine his strong, big hands trying so hard to form them correctly. I could imagine his face, the shape of his body, his breath in my hair. . . .

I put the vellum away and tried not to think of it or of the hand that had written it. I tried instead to immerse myself in the building of the church and the life of the village.

Within a few days there was another festival, this one

for the harvest. The women baked tiny cakes, and the villagers placed them in the ground as an offering to the goddess of the harvest, whose name was Erce. Mother Landrada had told me stories of her as well. She said her name is pronounced "Earth" by some, and that she is one and the same with the earth.

Conwoin opened the festival with a prayer of thanks to the Holy King of Heaven for allowing the earth, or Erce, to give her fruits to all mankind. He assured me that the King of Heaven was the Christian God and not the god Woden of the ancient Saxons. I prayed that he spoke the truth, although I suspected he saw the two gods as one and the same. I had learned tolerance and patience by Isaac's example, however. I would try to build their faith in Christ on the foundation of their existing beliefs, as he had taught me. That kind of tolerance, I now knew, would serve me better than anger and destruction.

There was much to celebrate at the festival, for the harvest was bountiful. Isaac had to hire several men and women to help him gather his grapes, and it was clear there would be good wine and plenty of it. I even saw him smiling several times. He almost seemed happy during the nine-day Jewish harvest festival of Sukkot. I joined the household in those nine days of thanksgiving and took my meals with them in the temporary ceremonial booth made of tree branches they called the sukkah. I felt no reluctance to participate because the Book of Deuteronomy says God, who is our one true God, commanded the Jews to do this.

Besides the harvest festivals, there was, finally, the church to dedicate. It was a humble wooden structure and not of great size, but it included Isaac's wall, and it appeared as something beautiful to all of us. The facade was flanked by two symmetrical towers, and in between was an intricately carved door. I provided drawings for the carving, but they were not followed precisely. If one looked closely, the voluptuous figure of Eostre could be found, along with the wheel of the sun and crown of Woden.

I planned the interior of the church to resemble the magnificent plan of the chapel I'd seen at the palace in Aix-la-Chapelle, with the central nave ending in a semicircle apse. There was no dome, however, and no murals, goldwork, or tapestries. They would come later and might never be as grand as the artwork in the church at Aix-la-Chapelle or even that in the humble church at Münster-Bilzen. They would most likely be the work of artisans in the village and would probably include some of the pagan symbols, but I had faith that all of it would eventually lead to the one true God.

After the harvest festival, Conwoin sent a man to the bishop at Dorestad to ask for a priest and to fetch the bishop for the consecration.

"The church must have a name," Conwoin said to me, "and since you have taught us well your methods for bountiful crops and made us strong in the faith, you must give her a name."

I knew, of course, that other missionaries of Christ who set out to build a church do so with a name in mind for its consecration. I thought myself unworthy of choosing the saint to be honored, though.

"Can't we leave it to the new priest to decide?" I asked.

Conwoin would not hear of it. "What will a stranger know of our lives? Or of what has gone into the building of this church? No, you must give her a name."

I told him I must pray first, and, at his insistence, promised him I would provide the name by the time the new priest and the bishop came to Temsche.

They arrived in the middle of the week, on the day the Saxons call Wodensdaeg, and the consecration ceremony took place the next day. It was the most beautiful day of my life. The air was autumn crisp and the sky a bright blue. Almost everyone in the village came for the solemn consecration and was on their best behavior. I was filled with happiness when I saw each one genuflect to honor the Host and then to receive it as pious Christians. The priest, a young man from Normandy, would learn just how pious they were soon enough, and I could only trust in God that he would be able to cope.

The church at Temsche was dedicated to Our Lady of the Nativity. It was a name that encompassed the foundation of the faith and the hope of their future.

That night, as I prayed the final office of the day, I realized that I had completed the circle of the year. I had arrived on a cold day in autumn, and now autumn had returned, but with more gentleness. It was time for me to return to the abbey at Münster-Bilzen and let Mother Landrada know my decision. It had not come to me easily, but now I knew with certainty that I would become a bride of Christ.

"Leave? You cannot leave." Judith was near tears when I announced my intentions just before we broke our fast the next morning. "We need you, and we have all learned to love you."

"I'm happy to have your love, and I will hold it in my heart always," I said, "but if I have done my job well, I have taught you not to need me."

"When?" she asked. "When will you leave?"

"I must return before the snow falls, a lesson I learned when I first came to you."

Her eyes lit up. "Then you will have time to—"

"I will leave tomorrow."

"Tomorrow? No! You can't. You mustn't." She began to weep and ran to me, encircling me in her arms and clinging to me.

"Yes," I said, stroking her head and her lovely dark hair, "it is what I must do."

She pulled away a little to look at me. "But why? Where will you go?"

"I will go back to my abbey. I will take my vows. I will serve our God as a bride of Christ."

I wept as well, and so did Josep, a little. We had learned to love one another, and we had become a family. I would miss them, even Isaac, who sat at the table eating his goat cheese alone and refusing to look at me. I felt compelled to speak to him.

"Isaac, I thank you for what you did for the villagers. Repairing the church, I mean. You truly did create a miracle."

He refused to respond or even to look at me, and although I wanted to say more to express my appreciation, his silence intimidated me to the point of making me mute.

The next morning I slipped away just before dawn. I was wearing shoes Judith gave me. They were her only pair, but she insisted that I would need them for my long journey, and she promised me she would have another pair made for her before the snow fell.

There was no freezing rain this time, as there had been a year ago when I arrived. There was only a skimming of frost that turned blades of grass to patches of gossamer shimmering in the morning mist. It was a coward's leavetaking. I had learned to love not just Josep's family, but all of the villagers, and I knew a more public good-bye would be too hard for me. They wouldn't be entirely surprised to see I had gone, however. I had told them a month prior that my time with them was coming to an end.

As I walked toward the gate I remembered that it had been a misty autumn morning like this one when I first saw Charles riding out of the forest with the stag thrown across his horse. Memories like that, of the things he said, the feel of his touch on my arm, the sound of his voice, still came to me at times, unbidden, but I'd become more adept at pushing them aside. He was so real to me now, though, as I walked into the mist, that I found it impossible to push away thoughts of him.

I could see him, phantomlike, riding toward me with the hooves of his horse hidden in the white clouds that clung to the ground, so that it looked as if he rode on air. I wanted to run to him, to have him sweep me up to ride with him on his great horse, but I closed my eyes until I was finally able to force the vision away.

I had not reached the town's gate when I heard my name called. When I turned, Isaac stood a short distance away. He looked small and wizened, wrapped in his hooded cloak.

"I knew you would leave us." He spoke in his usual disgruntled tone, making his words come out as an accusation.

"Yes." As always, I was a little intimidated by him.

"The villagers, the goyim, were right, you know. You were sent by God."

"It has always been my hope to be used by God as his servant," I said, finding myself surprised to be talking to him.

"The God of Abraham," he insisted.

"The God of Abraham," I said.

"See that you don't forget that."

"I never shall."

He looked down at his hands briefly, the only time I'd seen even the slightest sign of insecurity. When he raised his head again, he said, "I won't tell you to be careful on your journey, since, if a person is destined to drown, she'll drown in a spoonful."

I nodded and turned to leave.

"Amelia!"

"Yes," I said, turning back to him.

There was a long pause. "Thank you," he said.

My instinct was to go to him and kiss his cheek in a gesture of affection and farewell, but he didn't give me the opportunity.

"Go with God," he said and hurried away from me.

I whispered a prayer for God's blessing on Isaac and the entire village, then walked through the gate onto the open road.

My plan, as I took my first step on that road, was to be in the village of Drest by nightfall, where I hoped to lodge for one night with the Stavelots and be on my way again.

I walked for several hours before I saw the strange wooden boat in the river. The carved head of a dragon on the bow bared its teeth in the morning sun. On the shore a short distance ahead of me I saw three men with rugged beards and strange horned helmets.

At the same time I heard a scream and saw them fling a woman to the ground and start to undress her. One of the men looked up, saw me, and came toward me.

18

THE PALACE AT REGENSBURG

SPRING–AUTUMN 795

Charles

The great hall of the palace was dark. The entire world was dark, or so it seemed to Charles. Black clouds grumbled with the heavy weight of the rain they had yet to drop, and the air was unusually humid.

It was midday, so no one had thought to light the candles in the great hall, and Charles, his mood as dismal as the day, had no inclination to do it himself, or even to summon a servant.

He sat in front of a hearth where the fire had long since burned to embers, holding his injured shoulder stiffly, with the elbow of his good arm propped on the arm of a chair and his chin resting in his hand.

The palace at Regensburg was not one of his favorites. It was only a few years ago that he captured the town and made it part of his kingdom. The palace was hastily built and not nearly as beautiful as the one at Aix-la-Chapelle. Neither were there any of the warm natural springs that fed the baths at Aix. The Regensburg palace was Fastrada's favorite, however, since it was closest to her homeland, and she had spent as much time there as possible, even in the winter months, when the town and the forest surrounding it were buried in snow. She had died at Regensburg, and it was always her wish to be buried there.

Fastrada's wish was granted. She was buried on the palace grounds after a funeral Mass within a few days after her death last winter. The royal funeral, which had to wait until the king arrived, had just ended a few hours earlier. It took several days for all of the magnates to assemble, and now that they were here, they would not leave for several more days.

Counts Milo and Theodulf, as well as the Duke of Friuli, the governor of Bavaria, the Archbishop of Reims, and several princes who were members of the royal family insisted upon a council meeting. They had agreed to wait until tomorrow to begin the meeting, because of the funeral.

There was no doubt that he did mourn her death, as he did any mortal's, and he was sorry their relationship could not have been closer. He regretted, too, that she had not been happy as his queen. Perhaps she could have been if she'd borne him sons who might someday ascend to the throne. Charles found it impossible to grieve the lack of sons from her, however, since he had three surviving sons from Hildegard. Any more would only complicate matters of dividing the kingdom.

It wasn't Fastrada he thought of now as he sat alone in the darkened room, however. It was Amelia. He'd had no word of her or of the messenger he'd sent with a letter to her. He wished now that he'd never written that letter. If she ever did receive it, she would think him a fool and laugh at his awkward attempt at writing.

Yet he couldn't imagine her laughing at another's expense. Still, she would think him ignorant if she ever saw the letter. Would he ever be able to face her again? When would he even have the opportunity? Matters of the kingdom demanded his attention, and he was stuck in Regensburg, and she was miles away in Münster-Bilzen Abbey.

Sitting in front of the open hearth as he was now reminded him of sitting with her next to the fire at Aix-la-Chapelle. He remembered how warm and cheerful the fire was compared to the nearly lifeless embers he now saw before him. He remembered how lively their conversation had been. How they had laughed. How he had wanted to kiss her.

It puzzled him that almost everything in some way reminded him of her, to the point that he felt as if a curse had been placed upon him. Yet he would do nothing to rid himself of the curse, even if it had been in his power. He *wanted* her in his mind and in his heart.

Perhaps this was what it meant to love a woman. He had, of course, loved and respected his wives, particularly Hildegard, who was wiser than the others and equally as loyal. He'd felt a lusty attraction to all of his concubines, at least for a limited time. What he felt for Amelia included and went beyond all that he'd ever felt for those women. It frightened him sometimes to think of what power she had over his emotions. Nothing could make him more sublimely happy than to be in her presence, and nothing could make him more twisted with the pain of longing than her absence from him. He wanted to leave now and ride to Münster-Bilzen to find her, but his duties compelled him to stay in Regensburg.

The next morning, after a sleepless night, Charles was once again seated in the great hall of the palace. This time a fire in the hearth warmed the hall, and the light from the outside was plentiful, so there was no need for candles.

"I fail to see, Your Majesty, how you can consider the Avars defeated." Count Milo fingered the intricate gold hilt of his sword as he spoke. The sword was ceremonial, Charles noted, and had never been used in battle.

"Their army is diminished," Charles said. "We haven't suffered an attack from them in more than a year."

"There is still booty to be had," the Duke of Friuli said. "Surely you can't deny that, my lord."

"More booty?" Charles frowned as he lounged in his chair. "We've already brought home more gold and silver from their treasury than from any other enemy. And rich tapestries . . ." He pointed to an example of woven silk hanging on the wall. "I know many of you also have camels and Arabian horses."

"True, true, Your Majesty," Count Milo said, "but there are more, even richer spoils."

"Milo is correct," said the Archbishop of Reims, "but I, not being one who is overly fond of earthly treasures, would point out that it will take another battle to defeat the Avars for good and stop for eternity their aggressive actions to overtake the kingdom."

Charles turned his gaze toward the archbishop as he spoke and noted his robe embroidered with gold thread, the rings on his fingers, and his jowls, grown heavy from the rich food he'd swallowed. All of it belied the archbishop's claim that he was not overly fond of earthly treasures. Still, his point was well-taken. One more offensive against the Muslim warriors could stop their aggression forever.

"I fought with you at the Battle of Pannonia against the Avars, Your Majesty," the governor of Bavaria said. "I remember how brave and fierce you were. How the enemy fell at our feet like flies because you inspired us with your bravery. Another battle with equal zeal would protect the kingdom from them forever."

The Battle of Pannonia. Charles remembered it well. It was six years ago when he'd executed that campaign against the capital city of the Avars. He'd spent a long time in preparation, picked the best and bravest of his army, and fought with greater spirit than he had any other battle, except, perhaps, some he'd waged against the Saxons. His fervor had cooled, however, now that the greatest challenge had been met, and he'd won glory and honor for himself. He was content to leave the fighting and the glory to Carloman, his son.

"The Muslims are particularly resistant to baptism, Your Majesty," the archbishop said. Charles had failed to hear the first part of his statement.

"They are indeed," the king replied, knowing that the need to convert the Avars should, above all else, give him the will and passion to fight. But it did not. Perhaps it was because his will and passion were consumed with Amelia, although he could never admit that to anyone but himself.

In the end, Charles consented to the battle. It took him until well into the summer to prepare. He met with generals and with his son, Carloman, who would lead the battle. He sent word to wealthy landowners who would make up the elite side of the army and provide the peasants who would join them. He met with them again to discuss preliminary plans for distribution of the spoils that were sure to come.

"You've considered marriage again, of course," Count Theodulf said during one of the meetings. "I should think an Almannic or perhaps another Germanic woman like Fastrada would serve the kingdom best."

It wasn't an unusual hint. Almost every member of his court had pressured him to marry again, and each had a suggestion for a bride from a region that would serve the kingdom best. The pope had been among the first with a recommendation.

"We suggest a marriage that would provide an alliance with Almannia with the purpose of strengthening the southern borders of the kingdom," the pope had stated in a dispatch sent in early summer. His interest in securing the southern border would serve His Holiness well, since it would strengthen the buffer between Rome and any enemy who might sweep down from the north.

The governor of Almannia offered his daughter, Liutgard, whom Charles had never met.

"I will consider it," was all Charles would say in reply. However, he had little time to do so before another crisis demanded his attention.

The crisis occurred shortly after he left Regensburg to go to his palace in Paderborn. He went there, accompanied by Alcuin, to secure a group of noblemen for his army. Alcuin entered the palace while Charles spoke with the men.

"What is it?" Charles asked as soon as he saw him. He knew Alcuin would never interrupt a conference needlessly.

"A dispatch, Your Majesty," Alcuin said, handing it to him.

Charles glanced down at the letter. One of his emissaries in Rome had sent the dispatch informing him that Pope Leo had been kidnapped by a group of administrators favored by the late Pope Hadrian.

"Paschalis," Charles said, looking up from the letter.

Alcuin nodded. "Your friend Paschalis is no doubt behind the abduction."

"Send word to the emissaries in Rome immediately to

secure the pope's release," Charles ordered Alcuin. When Leo was elected pope he'd sent Charles the keys to the tomb of Saint Peter and the banner of the city of Rome. It was a way of confirming that he considered Charles the protector of Rome.

Weeks later, Charles received word back from the emissaries that they had secured the pope's release; on the same day a dispatch arrived from Paschalis asking for a council of both sides before the king so that he could hear both parties.

Charles scowled. "I don't want to go to Rome. I'm weary of traveling." He didn't add that his plan had been to leave Paderborn as soon as possible to go to Aix-la-Chapelle and Münster-Bilzen Abbey to find Amelia.

"Then assemble the delegates here in Paderborn," Alcuin said. "Hear both sides, and in the meantime I will begin research for you on the matter."

Charles agreed and allowed Alcuin to handle the details. Alcuin's council in political matters was always wise and carefully thought out, in contrast, Charles remembered with a sigh, to his abysmal insight into the female soul.

Pope Leo had grown so thin his body seemed lost in the rich folds of his white robe. His eyes were dark orbs lost in dark pools, and his skin was the color of weathered wood. Charles had never seen him look so decimated. His weeks in exile at the hands of his detractors had not served him well.

The pope sat in the throne room of the Paderborn Palace, hands folded and thumbs twitching, while his enemies presented the case against him.

"I have here a letter from the Countess of Monte Cielo describing in detail how this Leo, the so-called pope, lured her into adultery and then committed perjury before the magistrates by denying it." Paschalis waved the letter before the king and shook it as if he might shake more of the pope's sins loose. "I implore Your Majesty to reject this man who is not fit to fill the shoes of his worthy predecessor, and to remove him from the throne of Peter." Paschalis spoke in a voice that trembled with passion.

Charles knew Paschalis well. The late Pope Hadrian was Paschalis's uncle, and Hadrian had been among Charles's closest friends. Since Hadrian's death a few years earlier, Paschalis had lost much of his influence with the papacy, however, so he had good reason to want Leo off the throne.

Charles had become as fond of young Paschalis as Hadrian was. It was clear now that Paschalis hoped to use their friendship to accomplish his goals.

When the pope's defenders presented their case, they called upon a rule of law written two hundred years earlier, stating that the pope was not to be judged by anyone. He'd heard that argument before—from Alcuin, who had managed to present it in a way that was even more mind-numbing than the current defenders.

In spite of his distraction, Charles forced himself to

examine both sides of the argument, and endured several long discussions with Alcuin. He considered the fact that Leo had been lawfully elected pope, as well as the fact that he, as king, had already recognized him. He considered the accusers' motives and the questionable origin of the letter accusing the pope of adultery and perjury. On a night in early autumn after a long, tedious session discussing all points with Alcuin, he came to the decision that Leo would remain pope.

The decision made him feel relaxed and free for the first time in months. With the hearing behind him, he could leave soon for Münster-Bilzen Abbey, where he would find Amelia and ask her to be his wife. There was nothing standing in his way now. He was widowed, and she had not yet taken her vows.

They could return to Aix-la-Chapelle to plan the wedding. That would put an end to the constant and annoying admonitions from his advisers that he should take a wife.

He was enjoying the feeling of decisions well made as he prepared for bed. Before he was under the coverlet, a servant knocked at his door with a message from the pope, who, since the hearings began, had been lodged a few rooms away in the palace.

"His Holiness wishes me to convey to you a point for your consideration," said the messenger, a young man whose black hair was held in place and made shiny by a heavy coating of oil. He stood before the king dressed in the elaborate manner peculiar to Rome.

"Please ask His Holiness to confine his points of argument to the hearings." Charles made no attempt to keep the impatience out of his voice.

"With all due respect, Your Majesty," the young messenger said, bowing low, "the matter His Holiness wishes you to consider is not related to the current proceeding."

"What is it then?" Charles tried to stifle a yawn as he spoke.

"He would like to offer you the empire, Your Majesty. When these proceedings are over and as soon as you can come to Rome, he will crown you emperor of the Holy Roman Empire."

Charles was stunned and could think of nothing to say.

"His Holiness says to tell you no reply from you is necessary at this point," the messenger said, "but he wishes you to come to Rome for your coronation as soon as possible after these proceedings end."

Charles stared at the messenger a few seconds longer before he finally managed to speak. "Tell His Holiness you have delivered the message," he said finally.

The king slept not at all that night. He had made his decision to restore Pope Leo to the throne of Saint Peter. But Leo, not knowing the decision, was attempting a bribe. He thought of sending for Alcuin, but he did not, knowing this was a matter he had to decide on his own.

His announcement the next morning was made without joy. Pope Leo was restored to his throne.

The king began the long journey to Münster-Bilzen the next day. An entourage rode ahead a few days to announce his arrival at Aix-la-Chapelle, where he would stop for a fresh mount. Before he reached the town that had grown up around the palace, he saw a crowd waiting to welcome him. Among those in the crowd were noblemen, as well as peasants from the countryside and nuns from the abbey at Münster-Bilzen. Amelia was not among them.

His first thought was that she was too ill to travel. Or worse, that she had died. He rode the next day to the abbey to ask Landrada about her.

The abbess was confined to her bed when he arrived. Her swollen face was the color and texture of worn yellow linen, and her eyes were faded and watery, as if they'd been boiled overlong.

"Amelia has gone," Landrada said in the blunt manner of the Saxons. Her voice was weak, and the words came out with an odd kind of gurgle.

Charles felt his heart leave his chest for a moment, not certain of Landrada's meaning. Did she mean Amelia was dead? Or that no one knew her whereabouts?

"She has made a journey to Temsche," Landrada added.

"Temsche?" He knew of the village, may have even ridden through it once when his men were building the fortress called Antwerpen. But why would Amelia go to such a desolate and uninviting place, where there was not even so much as a church?

"Temsche is at least a week's journey, and not one a woman should make. Certainly not alone." He sounded scolding.

"Forgive me, my lord, but it is exactly the kind of journey Amelia should have made. And she is not alone. God goes with her, as does Sister Adolpha."

"Two women alone? I'm surprised you'd allow such a thing." He still made no attempt to hide his anger.

"It is the will of God," Landrada said, and after a long pause, added, "I was told by a bishop who stopped at the abbey many months past that there is need of a church there. He said it was only two days' journey away."

"He lied to you," Charles said, even more filled with anger. "He must have known you would never send anyone if you knew it would take at least a week of walking."

"Perhaps you're right," Landrada said. "Nevertheless, it became Amelia's mission to help build the church. And there was something I hoped she'd find along the way."

"Something to find? You have only to ask, Landrada, and I will supply you with whatever you need. There is no need to send a fragile woman to—"

"Forgive me again, Your Majesty; it was Amelia, not I, who had a need, and it is something you cannot supply her."

Charles gave an indignant snort. "I can supply her with anything she wishes."

"Then your knowledge and power are indeed superior, my lord," Landrada said, "because Amelia herself knew not what she wanted. And you are the cause of this indecision in her."

"I?" He might have scoffed at her had he not been so puzzled.

"You have caused her to fall in love with you, Your Majesty." Landrada paused and placed a hand on her chest, as if that might somehow help her labored breathing. "Before she met you, Amelia was on her way to taking the veil as a bride of Christ. Then, although she knew she could never be your wife and certainly not your concubine, she was afraid that her love for you would distract her or somehow make her unfit for her religious calling. It is my belief that this mission will help her see her way."

The king heard little more after Landrada said that Amelia was in love with him. Could it be true? Could it be that she longed for him and needed him as much as he longed for and needed her?

"When did she leave?" he asked.

"It was autumn last," Landrada said. "She will be back soon. I am sure of it. I will see her again and know her decision before I die."

"Tell me her chosen route," Charles said. He saw Landrada hesitate before answering, but in the end she obeyed her king, and well she should, he thought. It was he who had given her the position of abbess of Münster-Bilzen to appease her father, a Saxon chieftain who had betrayed his countrymen and helped Charles win a battle against them.

Charles set out immediately for Temsche. He would go to the abbey at Uslar, where Landrada told him Amelia had planned to stop first. He would ask about her there to make certain she'd made it that far, or to see if by some ill twist of fate she'd died along the way.

19

THE ROAD TO DREST AND BEYOND

AUTUMN 795

Amelia

Two of the men grabbed my arms and pulled me toward the woman and the man on top, who was now pumping himself into her. Just as we approached, the man finished with a loud groan and rolled away from her.

It was then I saw the woman's face.

"Brunheld!"

She looked at me with frightened eyes, but before she could speak, another of the men fell on top of her, pumping his body and raping her in the same manner the first man had done. At that moment, my body hit the leaf-covered ground with a painful thud, and one of the men was hovering over me.

Brunheld screamed something in a language I had never heard, and the man backed away from me, staring at me with a frightened look. Even the man on top of Brunheld stopped his attack and stared at me. Brunheld cried out again, still in the language I didn't know. Immediately the three men fled, the one who had last been on top of Brunheld without his pantaloons.

I stood and tried to help Brunheld, but she pushed me away and got to her feet on her own.

"Run!" she screamed, this time in the Saxon language. "I told them you were Hel, the Vikings' goddess of death. They are afraid of you!" She still screamed at me, to make the men think she was afraid of me as well. "Run!" she said again as she turned to run away from me.

I ran through the forest until I saw the men ahead of me and heard them talking in loud, frightened voices. I stopped and hid behind a large rock until I thought they were gone. I was just about to start out again when I heard another loud scream. Brunheld's scream.

I ran toward her and stopped when I saw her and the three men in the forest, inland from the river. Brunheld was once more on the ground, and the men stood looking down at her.

My mind raced as I tried to formulate a way to help her. While I stood there, paralyzed with fear and indecision, the men turned away, leaving Brunheld and moving toward the wooden ship I'd seen earlier on the river. I waited a few more minutes before I crept as silently as I could toward my friend.

She was dead. Blood pumped in an ever-slowing rhythm from her throat where the men had slashed it.

I fell on her body and sobbed soundlessly, hoping not to attract the men. I felt the warmth of her seeping out with her blood and soaking into my robe.

I don't know how long I lay there, but I stood finally, knowing I had to go back to Temsche to tell Conwoin. I started for the path along the river that led to the village, but as soon as I reached it, I saw that another ship had been rowed up the river and was anchored behind the first ship. A dozen or more Vikings swarmed around the two ships. I could not return to Temsche without their seeing me.

I went back to Brunheld and sat staring at her lifeless body while tears rolled down my cheeks. She had given her life for me, and now all I could do was watch while flies swarmed around her body and dipped themselves in her blood.

A groan of agony escaped my throat, and I stood, looking for something to use for digging. I found a sharp rock and scraped away enough of the soil to make a shallow grave. I lost any sense of time as I dug and then covered her with the soil to save her from the flies, and finally piled rocks on top to keep animals away. I prayed for her soul the whole time I worked.

And then I slept.

The sky was full of dirty rags of clouds obscuring the sun when I awoke. I walked toward the river until I saw that both ships were still moored there, and there were even more men milling around them. I could not go back to Temsche.

I would walk toward Drest and find help. Madam Stavelot, if she was still there, would know who to tell about the body and how to get word back to Conwoin.

I was filled with grief as I walked, but I willed myself not to think. Finally numbness set in. My movements were methodic and indifferent, and my mind as blank as I could make it. I didn't want to think or feel anything at all. It was a two-day journey, but I didn't want to return to the hermit's abode, so I slept on a cold bed of dry leaves. The next day I walked again. I felt my soul spark when I reached the edge of Drest and saw lamps at the gates burning away the darkness and saw the spire of the church towering above the walls. Perhaps it was nothing more than relief, but it was enough to let me know my soul was not yet dead.

Picking up my pace, I reached the gates just before they were closed. The gatekeeper motioned for me to enter when he saw my filthy novice's robe and the cross that hung from my waist.

"You've been hurt, Sister!" he said, eyeing the blood.

Somehow I couldn't form the words to tell him about Brunheld. I could only look at him dumbly.

"I've no wife to care for you. She died in the winter. Perhaps I could take you to—"

"I have a friend here. Madam Stavelot. If I could—"

"Stavelot? The bishop's wife? She's gone to live out her life in an abbey. It's a pity, but a bishop can't have a wife around, can he?"

"She's gone to an abbey? Which one?" I was still having trouble forming words.

The man shrugged. "Wasn't privy to her plans now, was I?" He stared at me a moment, then shook his head. "Come with me," he said, taking my arm. "I'll take you to the bishop. He has servants aplenty to help you."

I allowed him to lead me toward the church. Next to it stood a fine big house so new the timbers still shone with their original color. The man took me to the back of the house and knocked on the door. A woman who must have been a servant came to open the door, and as soon as she saw me and the blood that stained my robe, she sucked in her breath in alarm.

"The devil is loose!" she said, hurrying toward me. "You, a woman of the church, and look what he's done to you!" She took my arm and led me to a corner of the kitchen where a simple straw bed stood. "Leave us!" She threw the words over her shoulder to the man who had brought me. "I'll see that she's cared for."

I tried to call out my thanks to him and at the same time tell the woman I had not been injured. I couldn't form the words.

The woman filled a bowl with water from a pot she had warming on the hearth and brought it to me. "Clean yourself," she said, "and give me your robe. I'll rid it of the stains."

I felt too faint to remove my robe, and the woman had to help me. To cover my nakedness, she wrapped me in a woolen robe such as a servant wears.

"Who did this to you?" she asked as she took my robe away.

"Vikings." My voice was hardly more than a whisper.

She turned back to me and made the sign of the cross. "Devils," she whispered. "When the bishop hears of it, he'll have the king send out an army. You can rest assured of that. They cannot do this to a nun."

"Not to me," I said. "Another woman. Brunheld."

"Yes, yes," she said, cooing at me as one might a child or a halfwit while she busied herself with some pots hanging on the hearth. "I know you don't want to think it happened to you. Must be easier to think it was someone else." She glanced at me again. "And you are young," she added. "Perhaps a virgin until this happened?"

I said nothing. Why was I not able to explain to her that Brunheld was dead, that she had been raped, not I?

"It's all right," she said. "You'll have a bit of mutton and some vegetables; then you'll sleep. I'll inform the bishop as soon as I can. I can't do it tonight, because he's entertaining a very important visitor. I'm not allowed to say more, but rest assured I'll see that you are avenged."

"No," I said. "I must not be avenged. I was not the one who . . . Brunheld . . . She's dead."

"Dead, you say? Who's dead?" The woman gave me an enormous slice of mutton and a cup of vegetables.

"Brunheld. They . . ." I wanted to say they had killed her, but the thought of it made me sick.

"There, there," the woman said when she saw how I

gagged. "Try not to think about it. Sleep. That will do you good." She took the food away and returned to help me into the bed.

"Sleep now," she said. "This is a fine bed, and the bishop keeps it for any who come to his door. I'll be in my own bed only a few doors away. You must call for me if you have need."

After she left, I lay in bed exhausted, yet unable to sleep. Dark visions assaulted me—of Brunheld being violated, Brunheld dead.

I heard an agonized cry and was surprised to realize it was my own. I trembled and cried some more. Finally, I sat up and raised myself out of the bed, then walked out the door and into the night. The ground was cold and damp on my bare feet, but I didn't turn back for my shoes. I wanted to go to the church and pray. Even if it was bitter cold at this hour, I knew it was the only place I could find solace.

The church was indeed cold, and dark as well, but a few candles burned near the altar. I made my way to the front and knelt there praying for God to cleanse my soul of the pollution that still surrounded me. I stayed for a long time until I felt a presence behind me. I had not heard the door open, yet I was certain something or someone had entered.

I stood and turned around. A shape loomed in the shadows, hesitating as if he was waiting for his eyes to adjust to the darkness. Then the form began to move toward me. I watched him move closer and closer until I saw his face. He stopped.

"My God! It's you!" he said.

"Charles?" I moved toward him, slowly at first and then faster until I was in his arms. I clung to him. Was he real this time? My head rested on his chest until he raised my chin and kissed me. I made no effort to turn my face away but returned his kiss with an eagerness I didn't understand, absorbing him while he absorbed me.

Finally I pulled away and laid my head upon his chest again.

"I was afraid I wouldn't find you," he said. "Landrada told me to stop at Uslar Abbey first, and they told me one of you had died and was buried there. I didn't know which of you . . . You're trembling," he said, stroking my hair.

I couldn't respond.

"What's wrong?" He held me a little away, his eyes a question. "Something has happened. Someone has hurt you."

Still, I couldn't answer, but he must have seen something in my face. He picked me up and carried me out of the church and into the bishop's house. There was no one in the great hall as we entered, no candles burning, no fire in the hearth. Without regard for the darkness, Charles walked through the room to a door and kicked it open. Candles flickered on a chest near the bed. He placed me on the bed, seated, and sat next to me, holding me in his arms.

"Tell me," he whispered.

"I . . . I couldn't help her," I said, burrowing my face in his chest.

"You couldn't help . . . ? Who, Amelia?"

I felt a great knot growing in my throat, and I was afraid I was going to be sick. It was not the contents of my stomach fighting their way out, though. It was the dark, fetid memory of what I'd seen. I couldn't hold on to it any longer. I pushed away from him and told him the story, trembling as I spoke.

He was silent for a long time after I finished, but he pulled me to him again and held me close.

"I'll send armed men to Temsche at first light," he said. "They'll find the woman's husband and tell him."

"But I should be the one who—"

"No," he said. "Not you. Armed men. It will be dangerous enough for them."

"But they won't know where her grave is."

"You will tell them how to find it." He held me away from him again and faced me. "Now that I have you, I won't let you out of my sight."

I wanted to tell him how impossible that was, but at that moment he placed a gentle hand under my chin and lifted my face to meet his.

Our lips touched for a moment, whisper light, and then he smothered my mouth with his warm lips. It was a gentle kiss this time, but he pulled away too soon, as if he thought I might be afraid.

"What you saw," he whispered. "In the woods. You must not think all men are so brutal with a woman. There are ways to . . . to love a woman. Ways that are gentle and wonderful. The way God meant for . . ."

I found my hand reaching up, and my fingertips caressed his face. He captured my fingers in his big hand and kissed them, one at a time.

"I never want to hurt you, Amelia. I never want to frighten you."

"I'm not frightened," I said. "Not now. Not with you." I lay down on the bed, and he lay beside me, our faces only inches apart.

"I want to tell you how miserable I've been without you," he whispered. "How I thought of you day and night these many months. How I longed for you."

I was spellbound by his nearness, and I wanted to be even closer to him to force away the horror and sadness of what had happened. But I wanted more than that. I had an odd and pleasant sensation I'd never felt before, as if my body were slipping away.

"I want to hold you," Charles whispered, "to speak to you of nothing but my love for you."

"Show me," I whispered. "Don't tell me. Show me." I wanted him, needed him to wash away with his love the horror of what I had seen.

"I will show you," he whispered. "The way I did after the maypole dance."

Our bodies melded together, and he taught me then what it is to love, gently and profoundly. He showed me how the act of love is in no way similar to the brutal act I had witnessed. I gave no thought to the loss of my virginity, as I knew a nun should do. Instead, I felt cleansed.

Afterward, I lay in his arms, and we talked of trivial things and things of great importance. Once, I felt him wince when I moved my head on his shoulder. He told me then of the great battle that had left him wounded, and how the wound never healed completely. That was the wound I'd known about in the dark tunnel, I thought. The one he'd alluded to in the letter. I didn't mention the letter, worried that he might be embarrassed by his awkward attempt at writing, and when he didn't mention it either, I knew that I was right.

I kissed his wound as a mother would a child's and told him of the little girl who was injured when the church wall fell. I told him about the bishop's wife and about Isaac and Judith and Josep and Conwoin and the earth goddess.

He told me how he had tried for months to set out to find me, and how just tonight he had gone to the church to pray for me when he found me in the darkness. He told me, also, of the pressure he was under to marry the Almannic princess. He spoke of the plot against the pope and of the pope's offer to make him emperor.

"Emperor?" I said, sitting up and looking down at him, astounded. "You've waited until now to tell me that? Something that could change the world?"

"I fear it was only a bribe," he said. "His Holiness thought it would make me rule in his favor." I could see the agony of conflict in his eyes.

"And did it?"

"I had already decided to rule in his favor. The bribe served only to put my sense of ethics in chains."

"Then it wasn't a bribe," I said. "You can take the throne with a clear conscience."

He smiled and reached to stroke my face. "And you will be my empress."

I laughed at his jest. "And what does a nun know of being an empress?"

"You are not yet a nun." His face had taken on a serious expression, and I realized his remark was not made in jest.

"I will take my vows when I reach Münster-Bilzen." My voice was unsteady.

He sat up suddenly. "Take your vows? Why?" There was an angry edge to his words. "You can be empress. You can be at my side always."

"That is not what I was meant to do." My voice shook as I spoke. I could scarcely bear to listen to my own words. I loved Charles with my whole heart, my entire being, but earthly love was not to be my lot. I knew that clearly now.

"You speak of what was meant to be? This is what is meant to be," he said. "*We* were meant to be. Together forever. Isn't that as clear to you now as it is to me?"

"No," I said. "It is not." I touched his cheek. "Our Lord has need of me."

He got out of bed, wrapped a blanket around him like the toga of a caesar, and strode to the window. Instead of opening the shutters, he stood there a moment with his back to me. He turned around suddenly, his eyes flashing.

"I could command you to marry me. It is my right as king."

"Yes," I answered quietly. "It is your right."

"Would you disobey your king?"

"Would you have me under those circumstances?"

There was a long silence while we looked at each other. "It is impossible for me to believe you do not love me," he said at length.

"I love you," I said. "As I have never loved before. I love you more than my own life."

"Then why . . . ?"

I rose from the bed and walked to him, took his hand, and cradled it in both of mine. "Because you are meant to be emperor, to make your marriages for the good of the empire, to use your wisdom to make just laws, to defend the faith. That is the way you were meant to serve God. I was meant to serve as a bride of Christ."

"I won't stop you from serving God. As empress you will be free to—"

"I cannot be empress." I looked up at him. "In your heart you know that. I am no Almannic princess, nor a princess of any kind. I cannot benefit the empire by wearing a crown."

"What do I care about the benefit of the empire? I love—"

"You care about the empire, Charles. I know that. God knows that, and you know it as well."

He looked at me again for another long moment; then he touched my face and let his hand linger there briefly before he turned away and walked out of the room and away from me, slowly and with a sadness that broke my heart.

Mother Landrada was near death when I returned to Münster-Bilzen. She sent for me as soon as she heard I had arrived.

"Did he find you?" She was too weak to speak above a whisper.

"Yes," I answered.

"You love him," she said.

"More than I can express."

She smiled and closed her eyes. "Did you find yourself as well?"

I reached for her hand. It felt cold and dry as I held it in both of mine. "Yes, Mother, I did."

It seemed to take great effort for her to open her eyes and look at me. She didn't speak, but waited for me.

"I will take the veil," I said.

She gave my hand a weak squeeze and signaled for me to leave.

It was only a few days later that I received the veil in a ceremony she was too sick to attend. She spoke to me when I was summoned to her room immediately after the ceremony.

"I should have taken the veil as you did," she said in a labored whisper. "You are wiser than I was. I thought there was still a chance. I thought my lover would . . ."

She closed her eyes and slipped away with a sudden jerk

of her last breath, and I never learned the true reason that she did not become a nun.

Life at the abbey became a muted frenzy as we scrambled to make preparations for Mother's funeral while at the same time we mourned. A messenger was sent to inform the king, who was once again at Aix-la-Chapelle. No one doubted that he would come for the funeral or that he would also announce the gift of the abbey to his daughter Bertha. It was not likely that she would accompany her father, but most likely would make the journey to the abbey later to introduce herself to us and to claim her new possession.

The king arrived the next day, but I was busy with so many details I didn't see him until he took his seat at the front of the church facing us just as the Mass began. I saw him seeking me out in the crowded church, and when he locked his gaze on mine, I smiled. He responded with a brief nod.

I forced myself to follow the ritual of the service and to listen to every word. At the end of the Mass, the king stood. I felt a bittersweet longing as he stood there speaking of Landrada, her exemplary service, his respect and affection for her.

"She was a woman of God who claimed nothing for herself except the privilege of serving God. She set an example for the kingdom by dedicating an abbey, not to personal gain, but to God only. As the abbey passes now to a new abbess, it is our desire that Landrada's tradition continue, and it is for that reason that I award Münster-Bilzen to the only one who is capable of continuing that tradition, Sister Amalberga, called Amelia."

I was in shock and scarcely aware that I was being pushed forward by arm after arm of my sisters until I knelt before the king. I rose an abbess.

Epilogue

Aix-la-Chapelle

Winter 814

Charlemagne

He remembered the day for the rest of his life—the day he walked away from her and into a world that would know him as the Holy Roman Emperor, Charles the Great. Charlemagne.

Alcuin was at his bedside the day he died, as was Einhard.

"Write this down, Einhard," he said. "And write it well, for you know I never mastered the art of drawing words on parchment."

"Yes, Your Majesty," the scholar replied. He took up his stylus and dipped it in the inkwell.

"I loved her as no other man has ever loved a woman," Charlemagne said.

"It is a fine tribute you pay to your late wife," Einhard said as he scratched the parchment with his stylus. "Since

Queen Liutgard didn't live to become empress, her family will appreciate this tribute."

"My wife?" Though he was close to the seventieth year of his life and now lay sick abed with a fever, his voice was strong. "It's not Liutgard I speak of, Einhard, although I would not speak evil of her, frail and dull as she was. Still, I did not love her."

"Forgive me, Your Majesty." Einhard rubbed his forehead in a nervous gesture as he spoke, leaving a streak of ink between his eyes.

"I speak of the abbess," Charlemagne said, willing himself to be calm.

Einhard looked up at him from his parchment. "The abbess?"

"The abbess of Münster-Bilzen."

"Ah, yes. Sister Amalberga."

"Amelia," Charlemagne said. His voice was low and quiet, and he seemed to be staring at something in the distance only he could see.

"You loved her?" Einhard asked, perhaps more surprised that the king would admit it than that he loved her.

At this Alcuin cleared his throat and shot a warning glance at the younger man.

"I love her still," Charlemagne said. "And so did you for a time," he added with a weak chuckle.

Einhard blushed. "Münster-Bilzen flourished under her leadership," he said in an attempt to move the attention away from himself. "The agricultural methods she perfected there have benefited the entire empire."

"It was she who healed the wound on my shoulder with her kiss," the emperor said as if he had not heard Einhard. "Had she not died when she was barely past her thirty-second year, she would heal me now."

"Am I to write that, Your Majesty?"

"Yes, of course," Charlemagne said. "You will write the story of my life after I am gone. You will write every detail, and especially of my love for Amelia, but you will leave out the battle with the Viking horde I fought to avenge the act against her friend. She was not pleased with that. Said an eye for an eye was not a Christian act. I admit I feel no particular pride in it now."

Einhard paused and looked up once again at the emperor. "Excuse me, Your Majesty, but that was one of your most glorious battles, especially—"

At the sound of Alcuin clearing his throat again, Einhard said no more but went back to his writing.

"I wrote her a letter once," the king said, "but she was too kind to embarrass me by admitting she'd read it. Such was her virtue."

"Too kind to embarrass you," Einhard repeated laboriously, still writing. He glanced up at the king briefly. "Shall I tell the story of her riding on the back of a great fish when she crossed the River Scheldt to reach Temsche?"

Charlemagne laughed. "Only a legend, Einhard—it was told in the hopes of securing her position as a saint, but include it if you must."

Einhard wrote for almost an hour, until the emperor

grew tired and wished to rest. He stayed at Charles's side as he slept, and in the warm stillness of the royal bedchamber Einhard himself fell asleep in his chair. The sound of the emperor's voice awakened him.

"You've come again, my love," the emperor said. "Yes, of course I'm ready this time."

"Your Majesty?" Einhard said, unable to make sense of the king's words.

There was no answer, and when Einhard leaned closer, he saw that the Holy Roman Emperor Charlemagne was dead.

Einhard completed his story of the life of the great emperor in the Year of Our Lord 830. It was well edited by the sages of the emperor's court, who persuaded Einhard of the proper legacy of Charlemagne. No mention of either the revenge battle against the Vikings or of Amelia was included.

The King's Nun

Catherine Monroe

A CONVERSATION WITH CATHERINE MONROE

Q. What inspired you to write about Saint Amelia?

A. First, it was the fact that she was a contemporary of Charlemagne that attracted me to her. There is precious little written about women in the annals of history, so I saw this as an opportunity to tell the story of an actual woman who lived at the same time as one of the great figures of history. I wanted to explore how women might have been affected by the events of the day. I also wanted to look at how life might have been different for women as opposed to men in a way that might help explain why women are so often left out of history books.

When I found a reference that suggested Charlemagne had been in love with Amelia, I knew I had the potential for an appealing story, especially if she was also in love with him. Since she was a novice and soon to be a nun, I knew there had to be inner conflict for her if she was in love with him. I knew, too, that a man as powerful as Charlemagne would not be easy to resist.

The more I read about Charlemagne, the more he intrigued me. He was intelligent and sincerely religious. He was ahead of his time in advocating that women should be educated and in some of the property laws and laws for individual rights he established, yet he was perfectly capable of casting out a concubine when she no longer served his purpose. He was gentle in the way he reacted to his children and his friends, even shedding sentimental tears as well as tears of grief. He was also brutal in that he felt justified in slaying anyone whose religion was different from his. In short, he was a great character.

Yet this book was to be about Amelia. I had to make her a great character, too. With almost no information available about her, and with some of the existing information being suspect, even by the Vatican, I had a challenge. That challenge made me want even more to write the book.

Q. *How do you go about writing a story about a real historical character when so little information is available?*

A. I had to rely on sources (mostly books and Internet sites) that gave me information about the daily lives of people in the eighth century, when this story takes place. Since Amelia spent virtually all of her life in a nunnery, I had to find sources that would tell me what life was like in a cloistered community in the late 700s. Then I had to imagine what life would be like for a woman under those circumstances. I had to take the little snippets of the real story that I could find—for example, Amelia's journey to Temsche to found a church—and imagine why she went, how she got there, what happened there, and most important of all, how it might have affected or changed her.

Q. *How much of the story is true and how much is fiction?*

A. I like to say that it's all true, although it may not all be factual. According to a report I found in my research, Amelia probably did reside at Münster-Bilzen Abbey, although her records in the Vatican apparently are mixed up with those of another woman by the same name and from the same area, but who lived several hundred years earlier than the Amelia of my story. Both became saints, so all of those parallels made the research confusing.

It is apparently true that the Amelia of my story made a pilgrimage to Temsche to found a church, although the account is shrouded in legend and tales of supernatural events that the Church can't verify. Neither can it verify that Charlemagne fell in love with her, although the legend persists. It is true that Charlemagne had people beheaded for not being Christian. It is also true that he favored education for women, that his son, Pepin, attempted to usurp him, and that Charlemagne had him sent to a monastery as punishment. Einhard really did write a biography of Charlemagne, which I have read. Many of the characters in the book are real people.

Q. *You seem to have done a large amount of research. Do you enjoy it, even when it becomes difficult, as it obviously was for this book?*

A. Yes, I enjoy the research at least as much as and sometimes more than I do the writing. The more difficult, the better, since, as I mentioned, I enjoy a challenge. I have always liked reading history and the detective work of searching for an obscure or controversial morsel. I get to do the thing I love and get paid for it.

Q. *Are you a historian or a history teacher?*

A. Neither. Until I became a full-time novelist, my career was in journalism. I worked for various newspapers in both small towns and cities. I did hard news, investigative reporting, and feature stories. That was a career that taught me how to dig for information, how to filter out the nonessentials, and how to check and double-check the facts. It also taught me the discipline of writing. Just try telling a city editor on deadline you have writer's block and see how much sympathy you get.

Q. *What would you say is the main theme of* The King's Nun?

A. The theme, I think, is destiny. I don't mean destiny in a passive way. The book is about learning to believe in oneself and creating one's own destiny. It's true that Amelia's destiny seems to have been decided for her when she was given to the abbey as a young child. However, Amelia's ambition began to shape her destiny. In the end, she actually gets to choose her destiny. She could have conceded to the king's wishes. While that would have satisfied one side of her life, it would also have limited her and left her less room to grow. Women in the eighth century were thought incapable of possessing wisdom or strength of character. I wanted to make the point that they did and still do.

Q. *Why did you choose a bittersweet resolution to the story?*

A. I didn't choose the resolution, really. I just accepted that it had to be that way as the story unfolded. Given the time in history that the story takes place, and given the personality that emerged for Amelia, there was simply no other way to end her story.

QUESTIONS FOR DISCUSSION

1. The book begins with Amelia seeing Charles riding toward her through the mist while Amelia herself is shrouded in mists. How is this a metaphor for the story? In what way did their first encounter portend their relationship? Is it significant that neither of them speaks during the ride to the abbey?

2. Amelia was given to the abbey by her parents as a child. Would she have chosen that life if she had been given a choice? Why or why not? Do you feel she was happy at the abbey? Or was she only accepting of her life because she felt she had no other choice?

3. In what way did Amelia begin to change while she was at Aix-la-Chapelle? Was there a beginning of change in Charles as well? Was Charles being cruel or merely self-serving by not telling Amelia he planned to make his daughter abbess of Münster-Bilzen?

4. How would you describe Amelia's relationships with other women in the story? Do you feel Mother Landrada should have told Amelia more about her own early life, in particular about her lover? In spite of her ambition, did Amelia see Adolpha as a better candidate for abbess? Was Amelia too ambitious?

5. Discuss the relationship of Amelia and Charles in its various stages. Charles was an avowed Christian. Did his attitude toward women seem in any way unchristian? Were Charles and Amelia wrong to consummate their relationship?

6. Where do you think Alcuin got his ideas about the proper treatment of women? Discuss Madam Stavelot's statement that women were defined by their relationship to men. Do you think it is true today that women are defined by their relationship to men? Madam Stavelot hinted to Amelia that all women might be better off in an abbey. Given a choice, would Madam Stavelot ever have voluntarily chosen that life for herself?

7. Did Amelia's faith grow or weaken as the story progressed? Did she do the right thing when she destroyed the likeness of the goddess? What, if anything, did she

learn from the pagans in Temsche? What, if anything, did she learn from the Jewish family?

8. Discuss the symbolism in the story. What did the mists imply? What was the significance of the red dress? What did Isaac mean when he spoke of foundations?